Meghna jumped out of her bed as she felt drops of water on her face. "What the fuck…?"

"Tch… Tch! Such language on the dainty lips of a lady and that too first thing in the morning? What has the world come to?" asked a lazily amused voice from her left.

Meghna turned her head to look at the giant standing next to her bed. But the voice was human enough. This man was taller than her brother who was six feet. It couldn't be Rahul, of course. He wasn't as broad or muscular as this guy standing next to her. Rubbing her sleepy eyes, she got up to take a better look and heard him laugh. Oh my God! It *was* Rahul. He was grinning from ear to ear, all set to spray her with water once again.

"Rahul, you devil," shrieked Meghna as she catapulted into his arms, thrilled to bits when he caught her in a bear hug.

ABOUT THE AUTHOR

Sundari Venkatraman is an Indie Author who has 63 books to her credit. These books have consistently featured in the Top 100 Bestseller Lists on Amazon Kindle, in both romance as well as Asian Drama categories. Her latest hot romances have all been on #1 Bestseller slot in Amazon India for over a month.

MEGHNA is a standalone romance novel written and published by the author. This kindle book remained in #1 Bestseller position on Amazon India for four months from its release.

Even as a child, Sundari absolutely loved the 'lived happily ever after' syndrome and she grew up on a steady diet of fairy tales, Phantom comics and Mandrake comics. It was always about good triumphing over evil and a happy ending after the protagonists surmounted all unexpected obstacles.

Once she entered her teens, Sundari switched her loyalties from fairy tales to Mills & Boon. While she loved reading both of these, she kept visualising what would have happened if there were similar situations happening in India; to local heroes and heroines. And of course, the joy of vanquishing the ubiquitous evil villains! Her imagination soared and she happily ensconced herself in a rosy romantic cocoon for many years.

Then came the writing—a true bolt from the blue! And Sundari Venkatraman has never looked back.

Books by Sundari Venkatraman

Standalone novels
The Malhotra Bride
Meghna
The Madras Affair
An Autograph for Anjali
Twin Torment
Finding Anya
Mr. Perfect
Man Friday
Her Prince Charming
Love in Agartha
Arjun's Penance
The Floundering Author
Ryan Finds a Bride
Tinder Loving Care
Shaan Gets Hitched
For Better or For Worse
Love… No Conditions Asked

Collection of shorts
Matches Made in Heaven
Tales of Sunshine

Marriages Made in India Series
#1 The Runaway Bridegroom
#2 Her Smitten Husband
#3 His Drunken Wife
#4 Her Secret Husband
#5 The Casanova's Wife
#6 Her Bohemian Husband

The Bansal Legacy Trilogy
#1 Simha International
#2 Rose Garden International
#3 Maharaja International

The Thakore Royals Trilogy
#1 The Marriage Predicament
#2 Tied in Knots
#3 The Wooing of the Shrew

The Groom Series Trilogy
#1 Groomnapped
#2 Gobsmacked
#3 Grounded

Written in the Stars Series
#1 Scorpio Superstar
#2 Leo's Desire
#3 Taurus Temptation
#4 Virgo's Krush
#5 Libra's Flame

Arora Iyers Trilogy
#1 Once Bitten Twice Lucky
#2 Heartthrob
#3 Call of the Heart

Dashavatar (Indian Mythology)
MATSYA: The First Avatar
KURMA: The Second Avatar
VARAHA: The Third Avatar
NARASIMHA: The Fourth Avatar
VAMANA: The Fifth Avatar
PARASHURAMA: The Sixth Avatar

The Princess Series (Historical Romance)
#1 The Passionate Princess
#2 The Rebel Princess

The Writer's Toolkit (Non-fiction)
Publishing Your Book on Amazon KDP

Bollywood Bros Trilogy
#1 Sing For Me
#2 Dance With Me

Romantic Shorts Series
#1 Chahti Hoon Tumhe
#2 Beauty is but Skin Deep
#3 Madeinheaven.com
#4 An Arranged Match
#5 The Reluctant Bride
#6 Shweta ka Swayamvar
#7 Pappa's Girl
#8 Red Rose Dating Agency
#9 Rahat Mili
#10 Reema's Matchmakers
#11 The Matchmaker's Dream

MEGHNA

SUNDARI VENKATRAMAN

FLAMING SUN

Notion Press Media Pvt Ltd

No. 50, Chettiyar Agaram Main Road,
Vanagaram, Chennai, Tamil Nadu – 600 095

First Published by Flaming Sun 2014
Printed & Distributed by Notion Press
Copyright © Sundari Venkatraman 2014 & 2023
All Rights Reserved.

ISBN 979-8-89026-888-4

Cover Illustration: Unaiza Merchant
Editor: The Book Club Editorial Panel
Beta Read by: Rubina Ramesh

DEDICATION

This one is for Venkat, my husband of 38 years

ACKNOWLEDGEMENTS

- I thank my sisters Jayashree & Lakshmi for their enthusiasm and encouragement
- A special thanks to Neelesh Gajanan Inamdar for giving me a detailed critique about Meghna. Thanks to him, I rewrote the book in its present form
- I need to thank Rubina Ramesh for being a guiding force and helping me with marketing my books. She also had a strong hand in editing Meghna. Moreover, she has been available for editing consultation round the clock.
- The Book Club needs to be acknowledged here along with its members—a number of bloggers and authors who have been kind enough to read and review my work
- How can I forget Amazon for the amazing self-publishing opportunity? Thank you, Amazon! You are the best!

PROLOGUE

Where the hell was Meghna? Rahul looked at the empty room, wondering if she was in the bathroom. But neither the fan nor the airconditioner was switched on. And the bed looked undisturbed, as if no one had slept in it.

He heard a flutter and turned to the dressing table where a sheet of paper was flapping soon after the fan came on. Rahul took the couple of steps to reach out and was astounded to see it weighed down by the opal ring that he had given Meghna that very evening. What the hell!

A frown puckered his eyebrows as he read the letter—yes, it was a letter and was addressed to Reema *Bhabhi*. Meghna had left without a word to him, making a farce of the wonderful evening they had spent together.

Bhabhi dear,

I'm joining Sanjay on his flight to Dubai tonight. Don't worry about me. I'm perfectly fine. I just feel this tremendous need to get away. Everything's over between Rahul and me as you saw for yourself. I will be back with Sanjay. I hope that Rahul leaves town by then.

Love you, Meghna

"Goddammit," swore Rahul with a vengeance. This was exactly what he had been afraid of. Rahul swore again as he left Meghna's bedroom, closing the door behind him with a crash.

Reema gave him a startled glance as she saw Rahul storming out of her sister-in-law's bedroom. She had been sitting curled up on the sofa waiting to have coffee with the two of them, unaware that Meghna was not in her room.

"The little fool. Why couldn't she have waited for me to return home? A couple of hours I turn my back and she ups and leaves. Don't I deserve a hearing at all? Do I get hung without even getting a chance to explain myself?" Rahul ranted and raved, his frustration building up by the second.

"Rahul," Reema's voice was confused. "What's it? Is Meghna asleep?"

"Asleep, my foot. Read this, *Bhabhi*." He thrust Meghna's note close to Reema's face.

"But..." Reema had a bewildered look on her face. But when she saw the black frown on Rahul's countenance, she buried her face in the letter, finding it safer, only to let out a horrified shriek as she came to the end of it. "Rahul," her voice cracked as she hugged the note to herself, tears streaking down her face.

Rahul had moved to the window, wondering whether he should follow his foolish young fiancée and her brother to Dubai when he heard Reema's strangled cry.

He turned around to find the even-tempered, calm Reema in an anguished state. He rushed across to her and shook her hard as she tried to speak while no sound emanated from her lips. She only made a keening noise as she sobbed. He put his arms around her to pull her close. He pressed her face against his shoulder rubbing her head roughly, hoping to calm her down. He couldn't understand what had brought on the spate of weeping.

"*Bhabhi*, please calm down." He brought his own temper and frustration under control. "I'm sure Meghna's okay. It's only two days. They'll both be back…"

Reema didn't allow him to complete the sentence as she shook her head vigorously. "Rahul, Sanjay called to say that his plane was hijacked."

Rahul stared at her. *Was she hallucinating? Too many hours without sleep might do that to someone,* he supposed. How could anyone call from a hijacked plane? He shook himself from his reverie and spoke again softly. "*Bhabhi*, let me get this clear. Did Sanjay call you?" Sanjay was Meghna's brother, Reema's husband, and Rahul's best friend.

Reema nodded while the tears flowed faster down her cheeks. Rahul was totally confused. She had been quite calm when she had opened the door for him earlier. There had been no phone call after that. He would have heard the phone ring otherwise. Sanjay had obviously called earlier. To tell her what?

"*Bhabhi*, what did he say? That his plane has been hijacked?"

"Yes, Rahul," Reema found her voice. "Sanjay had cancelled going on the hijacked flight by chance. That's why he called to assure me that he was safe. But…"

Light dawned on Rahul's dismayed face as he understood the reason for Reema's tears. Meghna was probably on the flight which Sanjay had missed. A tremor ran through his body as his imagination drove him crazy with fear.

The phone rang as if on cue. He pressed Reema down on the sofa before rushing over to pick up the receiver.

It was Sanjay. "Where's Meghna?" he barked, the anxiety coming across the wires.

"Sanjay," Rahul's voice almost broke with the strain, "I think she's on that wretched flight." Panic rose in his voice as he enquired, "Any further news?"

Sanjay's voice cracked as his hopes died with Rahul's answer. "Nothing good. They're terrorists, I believe. They're keeping us in suspense until further notice."

"Tell me exactly where you are. I'm coming over." Rahul turned to look at Reema pathetically as he listened to Sanjay's instructions before disconnecting the phone.

"You go ahead, Rahul," said Reema with false bravado. "I'll be fine. I'll pray for Meghna's safety." She gave him a small reassuring smile that didn't quite reach her eyes.

Rahul popped into his room to change out of his formal suit into a pair of jeans and t-shirt and left the flat, closing the door quietly behind him.

"This is captain Rathod speaking…"

Hey, that's not Sanjay, thought Meghna as she pressed the overhead button for the air hostess. When there was no response, she called out to the one who was standing further down the aisle.

"Yeh lady, shut your bloody trap or I'll blow your brains out."

Meghna was horrified to hear the extremely rude voice near her ear as she felt something metallic press against her temple.

Could it be… could it be…? Oh no! It *was* the muzzle of a gun, the light glinting against the metallic sheen. She was terrified to notice the horribly unkempt stranger holding it against her temple. If his voice had been guttural and grating, his face was worse. He wore his hair long and had a thick moustache and beard. He was awfully filthy and she wouldn't have been surprised if she had seen lice crawling over all that hair.

She gave vent to the scream that forced its way into her throat. She just couldn't stop it. The next moment she faced the sweetness of oblivion as the terrorist hit her hard against her temple with the back of his gun.

About a month ago…

The traffic didn't disturb Rahul's euphoric state as he drove home to Wimbledon from London. Even the incessant rain and slush didn't irritate him as it usually did while the Volkswagen's wipers worked furiously to keep the view clear.

He was still mulling over the afternoon's incident at the board meeting. The bank's board consisted of members over the age of fifty while he, at thirty, was the only young associate. It was always up to Rahul to bring fresh ideas to the table, which was usually met with strong opposition. While it took time, Rahul always managed to get his way to bring about changes in their Victorian way of handling business.

This time the battle had been about opening a new branch in what the board considered to be the wrong side of the tracks. Rahul's argument was that that particular area was becoming a hub for new businesses. It had been more than a year since he brought up the proposal with his father Shyam Sinha and a couple of other board members backing him. He kept bombarding them with facts and figures of all the businesses happening there, hoping to wear out their resistance. Today, finally, the rest of the board had fallen in with his idea and the project had moved on to the next stage.

Rahul grinned to himself as he inched his car behind the tail lights of an Infiniti. In fact, he had been smiling to himself all evening, feeling triumphant.

He picked up his cell and speed-dialled Joe's number, using his Bluetooth to keep his hands free. "Hey Joe!"

"Hey, man. How are you? Long time, no see," said his best friend on the other end.

"Let's party tonight, Joe."

"Fantastic! Where do you wanna go?"

"Hmm… what about the new pub which was opened last month? Oh yes, Impact, at ten?"

"Right, man. I'll call Rita, Seema, Arwan and Bill. You'll catch the rest of the gang?"

"Great Joe, thanks. Knew you're the man for it," grinned Rahul, hearing the cheer in Joe's voice.

"Anytime, dude. Catch you soon."

Rahul rapidly made a few more phone calls to other friends. He was keen to party as the past few months had been all work, even during weekends.

He parked the car in front of the opulent twelve-bedroom house and got out of it, slamming the door behind him. He rang the bell long and hard before Ramsay, the butler, opened the door to let him in.

Yes, that's right, a real-life butler, in this day and age. Rahul's mother Rajni was pompous to the extreme and felt the compulsion to impress her snooty friends with her lavish lifestyle. Apart from the butler, she also made costly purchases worth thousands of pounds to show off to those same shallow-minded people. But of course, Shyam Sinha could afford that and more. What was sad was that Rajni lost interest in her possessions after her friends finished admiring them. While a few paintings were hung around the house, Shyam kept the rest of the paintings, sculptures and curios safely tucked away in a storeroom as investments. Father and son weren't too keen on turning their home into a museum.

Rahul was absolutely convinced that he was exactly like one of those priceless objects to his mother. This had in no way deterred him from growing up into an extremely secure and confident young man, thanks mainly to his father Shyam who worshipped the ground his son walked on. Within a couple of years of marriage, Shyam realised how his wife was and began to ignore her once Rahul was born. And he simply adored his only child.

The Sinhas used to live in India and later had moved to London about a decade ago. Shyam had always been a banker. Rahul completed his CA in Mumbai—living with his friend Sanjay and his family—before moving to London to join his father's bank. He treated the house more like a hotel much to his mother's annoyance. But then, she had no hold over her only son.

Rahul walked into the hallway and said, "I wouldn't be home for dinner, Ramsay. Don't wait up for me." He smiled at the old man, patting him on his shoulder.

Ramsay felt a fierce sense of loyalty towards Shyam Sinha, which he extended towards the son of the family. He continued in this job only because of the men of the household who treated him with great affection. His reputation as a butler was such that every rich family would have received him with open arms.

"Yessir, Mr. Rahul," answered Ramsay.

Rahul was bursting to share his wonderful news with someone and decided to speak to Sanjay, his closest friend.

Sanjay Srivastav and Rahul had been to school and college together. Sanjay had gone on to become an airline pilot with an international company. His mother had treated Rahul like her own son. Sushma had been widowed at a young age when Sanjay had been ten and his younger sister, Meghna, two. They were from the middle-class but Sushma's heart and home had always been large enough to hold Rahul as well. These days, Sanjay was happily married to Reema and they had two kids.

Rahul lifted the phone and dialled the Mumbai number. The phone receiver was lifted after only two rings by Sanjay's baby daughter, Sasha. She was almost four. It was eleven at night in India and the little brat was still wide awake.

"'ello," came the baby voice across the phone line, making Rahul smile with joy.

"Hello, Sasha darling, this is Uncle Rahul. How are you, sweetheart?"

"Unca Ra'ul," the voice giggled. Sasha knew Uncle Rahul from the pictures her parents had showed her on their laptop and cell phones. Rahul could hear Reema call out to Sanjay as she scuffled with Sasha to persuade her to give up the telephone receiver.

"Give the phone to Mamma, sweetheart," Rahul requested in a gentle voice.

"Yes," the child passed the receiver to her mother.

"Hello, Rahul. How are you?" The two of them were good friends and exchanged messages regularly.

"Hi, *Bhabhi* dear. I'm just great. And you? Beautiful as ever, I'm sure."

"Flatterer! What's up? Have your old cronies allowed you to have your say at the bank or should I come over and give them a piece of my mind?" asked Reema, fiercely loyal.

Rahul grinned as he listened to her rapid-fire chatter. "The board has finally agreed to my suggestion, *Bhabhi*. I'm just too thrilled," he yelled down the phone line like a small kid.

Reema shouted back her, "Congratulations!" with equal enthusiasm. "That's just super! But even better will I feel on hearing the news of your marriage."

"But, *Bhabhi*," Rahul sighed dramatically, "did you know that I so wanted to marry this lovely girl I met a few years back? She spoilt me for anyone else."

"Oh, Rahul," cried Reema eagerly, "you never said anything before. Who's this? What's her name? Where's she from?"

"The sad thing is my closest friend married her," he uttered in a pseudo-woeful voice.

"Idiot!" Reema caught on, laughing out loud. Rahul was an absolute tease.

Rahul's guffaw sounded loud as Sanjay took the phone receiver from his wife.

"Rahul, *mere yaar, kaise ho?* It's been a while since we heard from you."

"I know and I'm sorry, Sanjay. I'd been busy with you know what."

"Oh, yeah, Reema keeps me posted. Congrats! I'm very happy for you. Do tell me when you're coming down to Mumbai. You haven't even met my kids yet. You aren't going to wait until they are adults, are you?"

"I'll come over soon; will surprise you guys."

"Can't wait for that."

"Sure Sanjay." Rahul chatted some more with his best friend before signing off. "Catch you soon, bye."

"Bye and take care," responded Sanjay.

Rahul had a satisfied smile on his face as he got ready to go out.

ahul ordered a cab to pick him up at 8.30 as he planned to get drunk at his own party.

Some of his friends were already at the pub when he reached there. They waved to him as he walked up to where they were seated. Three tables had been pulled together to accommodate all of them.

Rahul could see Rita eyeing him from her corner seat as she patted the empty one next to hers. His honey brown eyes moved away from her, pretending not to notice her invitation. He walked up to Joe and settled his six-foot-three-inch frame into the seat next to his best friend. Running his fingers through his dark curling hair, he pushed back the strands which had fallen forward on his wide forehead. He smiled at each one of them, greeting everyone exuberantly.

People shifted around and Rahul found Rita right next to him, with Seema on her other side. He heard Rita whisper "Sexy," to the other woman but once again pretended not to notice. The other men didn't seem to mind the girls hovering around Rahul like bees to a honey pot.

He asked Joe, "Where are Sam, Bets and the others, *yaar*? Are they coming?"

"Yeah, man. They're on their way."

"Come on, then. Let's start the fun."

They all ordered another round of drinks and starters.

Rita asked Rahul, "Dance?"

"Sure, why not?" He went along with her, swaying to the music. Rahul loved to dance. It gave him a great sense of freedom gyrating to the pulsating music. The beat got into his blood and he danced away, feigning ignorance of his partner's hungry glances in his direction.

Rahul was aware of Rita's attraction to him since the time they met three years ago. He had managed to keep her at arms' length, treating her exactly as he would Bill or Joe. He ignored the deep sigh that rose from within her and continued to dance. He could sense Rita's excitement when the music slowed down to a waltz. He immediately stopped dancing and insisted on guiding her to the bar. "You must be thirsty after that fast number," he smiled, refusing to acknowledge her gnashing teeth.

"Unromantic fool," she muttered, loud enough for Rahul to hear. Not that he reacted to that either.

Rahul appeared blissfully unaware of Rita's irritation as he hummed the tune under his breath. He grabbed hold of two beers and thrusting one into her hand, took a long swig from his. "Hah! I needed that after the last two numbers. Enjoying yourself, eh, my Rita?" He gave her a friendly hug much to her annoyance.

Rita was very pretty, a golden blonde with widely-spaced dark blue eyes. But she seemed not to spark any interest in Rahul, at least not the kind she craved.

"Hey, Sab, Bets. Glad you made it. Where are the guys?"

"Parking the car," they chorused. Sabrina and Betty were going steady with Sam and Ronnie. Rita did her best to catch Rahul's eye as the other couples got engrossed in kissing each other. But he was too busy getting some drinks for the new guests. Amongst a lot of backslapping and joking, the whole gang moved towards the dance floor.

They danced the night away and Rita never got another private moment with Rahul, which was not surprising, actually. He made sure that he was never alone with her again that evening.

It was four in the morning when the party broke up. Rahul dropped Seema on his way and reached his own house at five, opening the front door and letting himself in quietly.

It was noon by the time Rahul came down the next morning. "Good morning, Rahul," greeted his mother in a surprisingly cheerful voice.

Rahul raised his right eyebrow sardonically, "Oh, morning."

"My dear Rahul," she drawled.

He scowled, hearing her saccharine tone. What did she want now? The eyebrow went higher.

"My darling son," Rajni continued, undeterred by the fierce expression on his face, "Congratulations!" she gushed.

"Thanks." The eyebrow stayed up, waiting for her to get to the point.

"Darling! I've organised a party tonight in your honour." Rajni pretended not to notice her son's lip curling in disgust. "Everybody who is somebody will be coming over. You know how successful my parties are." She clapped her hands in delight, proud of her entertaining skills. "Despite the short notice, I've managed to invite everyone and organise the caterers, decorators and musicians. Anyway, I don't want to bother your handsome head with details. Those are all my department." She sighed dramatically, as if she had done the cooking, cleaning, and decorating single-handedly. "You must make sure to be there. My friends can't wait to meet you. They're so envious of me. Sheila says, 'Oh Rajni! You're so lucky to have such a handsome and intelligent son.' I can't wait to catch the envy on their faces when they meet you today."

The truth was out, the real reason why his mother had spoken to him for the first time in months. Not that they had been quarrelling or any such thing. She only spoke to someone if she had a personal stake in it.

"Is Dad coming to the party?"

Rajni wasn't keen on her husband's presence at the get-together as she believed him to be a bore. Looking at her son's belligerent expression, she changed her mind and decided then and there that Shyam's attendance was a must.

"Yes, of course, dear Rahul," she drawled.

Her voice grating on Rahul's nerves, He simply gave her a nod before walking away.

"And Rahul." She continued when he stopped without turning to look at her, "Be ready by nine; the dress code's formal."

Rahul went into the kitchen to get something to eat. But the sight that met his eyes was startling. There were more than a dozen people cooking up a storm in the cavernous kitchen, preparing mountains of food for the evening.

Ramsay walked into the kitchen with an empty tray. "Good afternoon, sir!" he greeted his young master. Grasping the situation immediately, he said, "Where would you like me to serve your breakfast, Mr. Rahul?"

Rahul was relieved to see the butler. "Good afternoon, Ramsay. Can you please serve me in the garden? I'd love to have a typical English breakfast today. I'll have some hot coffee along with it," he said before stepping out of the kitchen via the back door. It felt so good to be out in the fresh air and Rahul stretched his arms high before sitting at the table that was set under a colourful umbrella. He opened that day's newspaper and got engrossed in it before the smell of sausages wafted towards him. His stomach growled hungrily as Ramsay set the tray in front of him. He thanked Ramsay before tucking into the eggs—sunny side up—and sausages with bread and hot coffee, made exactly the way he liked it.

As the affluent guests thronged the Sinha residence, Rajni was in her element, resplendent in a sequined chiffon sari, a brilliant pink in colour. Hired waiters walked around serving the guests with cocktails of their choice, fetched from the bar that was at one corner of the living room. A variety of snacks were carried around as everyone exclaimed over the lavish arrangements.

Rajni proudly introduced her son to all her so-called friends. Rahul put up with this for briefly before moving away towards his father who was talking politics with another unfortunate husband. Shyam held out his hand to his son, smiling. The resemblance between father and son was striking. They had the same determined chin and hard cheekbones. Only Rahul's eyes were like his mother's. Father and son shared a deep bond.

"Ah, Rahul! Come, my dear boy, meet Ramnik Arora." Shyam turned towards the gentleman next to him, "Ramnik, this is my son Rahul," he said.

Rahul shook hands with Ramnik Arora saying, "Hello, sir, pleased to make your acquaintance."

A vision sailed towards them, catching Rahul's eye. She had a vivacious personality, with black hair and eyes. She was wearing a black full-length sleeveless dress. As she moved, the dress parted on the left to show a slit up to mid-thigh. Rahul smiled at her. She walked up to them, slipping her arm through Ramnik's. At close quarters, her bright red, pouting lips and knowing black eyes turned Rahul's smile cynical.

"Shyam, Rahul, meet my only daughter, Aisha." Ramnik proudly introduced the young woman.

"Hello, Uncle." She shook hands with Shyam and turned her flirtatious gaze to Rahul,

"Hi, handsome!" So greeting him, she held on to his hand longer than was necessary.

Rahul looked amused as the older men excused themselves and moved on.

"Hello yourself," said Rahul.

"The name's Aisha."

"Hmm… mmm."

"I'm amazed that we've never met!" Aisha smiled at him invitingly, placing her right palm on his chest. "I would've never forgotten you."

Predatory!

He smiled back at her, his eyes crinkling at the corners, "Well, I wouldn't have forgotten you either." And he would probably run a mile away if he ever caught sight of her first.

"Let's celebrate." She dragged him towards the bar.

Rahul went along for want of something to do. He was bored, not caring much for high society gossip which floated all around him.

Aisha ordered a gin and tonic for herself while Ramsay passed Rahul his whiskey and soda. Her eyes narrowed speculatively as she watched Rahul as he looked around the room, his boredom obvious. She tapped him on his cheek to get his attention, "What's up?"

"Nothing," said Rahul, shrugging his wide shoulders as he sipped from his glass.

"I must congratulate you, Rahul! Your mother's so proud of your achievement."

"Thanks," Rahul gave her a half-smile, his eyes roaming around the room, looking for a way to escape from the clinging Aisha.

"Darlings," Rajni descended on the two of them along with some of her friends.

Rahul gave a curt nod, continuing to sip from his glass, not at all keen to get into a conversation with the bored socialites.

Aisha gushed, "Rajni Aunty, where've you been hiding your handsome son? No fair!" She pouted at Rahul's mother.

Smiling widely at her young guest, Rajni turned around to the others and asked, "Don't they look perfect together?"

Rahul jerked his head as if someone had chucked a bucket of cold water over him.

Aisha smiled widely, smug as a cat.

The other women nodded their heads vigorously, adding their own compliments.

Rahul switched off from the conversation surrounding him; one which he hadn't been involved in to begin with. He didn't hear the chatter around him as he turned his head this way and that, desperate to get away.

"Rahul," Aisha tried to claim his attention.

"Excuse me! Dad's looking for me. Here, Dad," he called out loudly before slipping away. He stepped through the French windows into the beautiful garden. A cool wind blew across, ridding him off the mental cobwebs. He was irritated with his mother for her crude behaviour, shuddering as he recalled the scene he had just left behind. He breathed deeply to control his simmering temper and took a couple of rounds. After calming down, he went to bed without bothering to say 'goodbye' to the guests. It was his mother's party anyway.

Rahul was up early in the morning. After his jog and swim routine, he went for breakfast at 8.30.

"Good morning, Dad," he called out cheerfully when he saw Shyam at the dining table.

"Good morning, Son." Shyam looked up from his newspaper with a smile on his face.

"Rahul, my darling boy, good morning! Where did you disappear to last night?" drawled his mother's voice.

Rahul's eyes widened. That was a first—Rajni up so early in the morning, that too, on a Sunday. Her day didn't begin before noon. He looked at his father enquiringly.

Shyam shrugged his shoulders before burying his face in the newspaper.

Rahul stared at his mother without responding to her greeting.

"Aisha was so upset when you didn't return to the party. Isn't she a charming girl? I think she'll make you an excellent wife. I accepted the proposal when her parents put it forward." She told her son with a smug smile on her face, seemingly unaware of the bombshell she had dropped.

Shyam came out of his newspaper once again and looked at his wife as if to check if she was serious. Though he said nothing. Rahul was big enough to fight his own battles.

"Do you want my opinion?" Rahul's voice was dangerously quiet.

"Oh, come on, Rahul! You must surely agree. The girl's beautiful and rich. She's much sought after. You can't find a better…"

"How come this paragon is still single?" asked Rahul, keeping a tight rein on his temper.

"That's because she has chosen to be. But Aisha's fallen flat for you," said Rajni triumphantly.

"No." Rahul's voice like a pistol shot.

"Rahul, listen to me…"

"No way! You stick to your shopping, friends, and your parties. Don't interfere in my life." Rahul bit the words out through tightly clenched teeth.

"How dare you? You're my son, my only child. Have you forgotten that I'm your mother?" Rajni screamed at the top of her voice.

"You gave up that right when you left me in Shanta *Mausi's* care when I was barely a month old. Don't you dare try to run my life now, after all these years," Rahul warned her again, his golden-brown eyes matching hers in temper.

"Shyam," shrieked Rajni. "Make your son understand that I can't go back on my word," she ordered. "You have to make him agree. He always listens to you," she implored.

Shyam gave her a benign smile. "In case you haven't noticed, our son is above six feet tall and all of thirty years. He's quite capable of finding himself a wife." He didn't elaborate further.

Rahul finished his meal and gestured to his father before leaving the dining room without uttering another word.

Rajni ranted and raved about ungrateful husbands and disrespectful sons.

It seemed not to disturb Shyam one iota. He calmly read through the paper from one end to the other, sipping his coffee before he finally got up to leave too.

"Shyam," Rajni clutched at his arm, her fingers like talons. "You haven't heard a word I said."

"I stopped listening years ago." He slowly removed her hand from his arm, dusted his shirt sleeve meticulously, shrugged into his coat jacket before walking away.

Rahul calmed down as he drove to the country club, his lips curving into a smile as he remembered the chilled-out manner in which his father had reacted during the drama. Good old dad!

His thoughts moved on to his mother. He had no feelings of bitterness towards her. She was what she was. But why this sudden crazy idea of getting him married? He shuddered at the idea of being tied to that man-eater who prowled around in the name of Aisha.

Thinking of marriage led him to thoughts of finding a suitable life partner, his mind going to his last day in Mumbai six years ago…

It was late evening and the flat was silent. Her mother's sudden death had come as a rude shock, and young Meghna was inconsolable. She had locked herself in her room and refused to open the door. Her brother Sanjay and his wife Reema had tried in vain to talk to her.

Rahul, Sanjay's best friend, had been like a foster son to Sushma Srivastava—Meghna and Sanjay's mother—who had suddenly died of heart attack. It was not just Sushma's children who were shaken, but Rahul Sinha too. Sushma had been the backbone of the family, bringing up her two kids single-handedly after the death of her husband fourteen years earlier. She had been a surrogate mother to Rahul as his own mother had never bothered with him.

He and Sanjay were friends since schooldays and Rahul was as good as a member of the family. When Sanjay couldn't get through to his sister, Rahul insisted that his friend and his wife should rest while he promised to tackle Meghna.

Rahul left Sanjay's bedroom and stepped into the rectangular hall in the centre, with two adjacent bedrooms on each side of the hall with a kitchen, a *puja* room and dining area. Sanjay's bedroom was on the left wing and Meghna's on the right, adjacent to what used to be her mother's. He knocked on Meghna's door lightly.

"Go away," was the muffled reply.

"Meghna, this is Rahul. Open the door."

"Go away," she repeated, her voice louder this time.

"Please, Meghna, I'll be leaving in a few hours." Rahul's voice beseeched her.

The door opened with a crash. "You're leaving?" Tear drenched grey eyes, innocent of make-up, glared at him accusingly.

Rahul stepped into the room before she could shut herself in once again, giving her a small smile.

"You haven't answered my question." Meghna glared at him autocratically.

Rahul's smile widened. "You very well know I'm leaving tonight for London, my dear Meghna, so why this flash of temper?"

"But Rahul, how can you leave now at this time? Mamma just passed away and you're also leaving…" Fresh tears coursed down her chubby cheeks as Meghna cried her heart out.

Rahul's face was also wet with tears as he enfolded her shuddering body into his arms. Meghna buried her face in his chest and cried her heart out. It was like a dam burst. Rahul held her plump body for he knew not how long, waiting for the pain to fade away with the tears.

Meghna gradually calmed down and stopped crying. Neither of them spoke for a long time as her body continued to shake with sobs. He stroked her dark head, glad that she was finally expressing her sorrow as she had simply clammed up and gone silent on everyone after the news of her mother's sudden expiry.

Meghna looked up at him to ask, "Can't you postpone your trip?"

"No, Meghna."

"But…"

"Mamma has gone. We've to accept that and continue with our lives."

Which sounded callous to the sixteen-year-old. "How dare you talk like that?" She shouted at him, straining at the arms holding her.

Rahul kicked the door shut. "I dare because it's the truth Meghna; accept the fact. Mamma had a good life. She was happy to see you all settled in this new home. Now let go of her."

"What's it to you? She wasn't your mother anyway." Unable to bear her own pain, Meghna turned offensive.

"Wasn't she?" asked Rahul sadly.

Meghna stared into his distressed eyes and regretted her rudeness. "I'm sorry, Rahul."

He gazed down at her swollen face with affection. "That's okay. Now promise me that you'll be a good girl. Don't shut Sanjay and Reema *Bhabhi* out. They love you and are hurting so much because you've been ignoring everyone. And also promise me that you'll study well and grow up into a wonderful young lady."

A sudden smile lit up her sad face. "Sure, Grandpa Rahul, I will."

Rahul tweaked her nose affectionately. She was so short that she barely reached his shoulder. She hadn't lost her puppy fat yet but had the beginnings of a great beauty. Her large grey eyes with long, thick dark lashes looked up at Rahul trustingly.

"Do you really have to leave tonight?" whispered Meghna. "I'll miss you terribly."

"I need to go, Meghna. My dad needs me to join at the bank. My studies are over. I don't have anything to keep me here," he pointed out reasonably.

Meghna continued to stare at Rahul with her tear-drenched eyes, at a loss for words.

She's still a baby, thought Rahul. But he was going to miss her awfully, too. They had grown very close over the years. He couldn't resist kissing the 'baby' softly on her mouth. He was surprised at the way her lips clung to his and immediately regretted his action. He pulled away after a small tussle. "Bye, Meghna." He released her and stood a couple of feet away. "And no more tears, please."

"I'm not a cry baby," returned Meghna, faking anger to cover up for her shyness.

"I guess not," grinned Rahul teasingly.

Meghna put her own small hand in his, saying, "Bye, Rahul and take care. I'll keep my promise.

He shook her hand solemnly and said, "Goodbye, Meghna."

After all these years, Rahul could still feel Meghna in his arms. He had kissed her innocent lips, forgetting that she was barely sixteen...

Rahul came back to the present as the traffic light changed from red to green. He touched his mouth in wonder as he had almost felt Meghna's lips against his. He shook his head, smiling to himself. Now why had he recalled that scene with Meghna at the mention of marriage?

When his father arrived at the club where the two of them played golf on Sundays, the first thing Rahul said was, "Dad, I'm going to Mumbai."

"Are you running away from your mother?" asked Shyam.

"You're joking, right? Come on, Dad, you know me better than that."

"I just wondered."

"Of course not. I was just thinking that I haven't met Sanjay in a long time. I've never seen his kids. I can afford to take a break now, I think."

Shyam looked at his son affectionately. "If anybody deserves a break, it's you, Rahul. Get on with your plans."

"Mom…" Rahul hesitated.

"Allow me to deal with her."

"Thanks, Dad," Rahul hugged his father before continuing with the game.

eghna jumped out of her bed as she felt drops of water on her face. "What the fuck…?"

"Tch… Tch! Such language on the dainty lips of a lady and that too first thing in the morning? What has the world come to?" asked a lazily amused voice from her left.

Meghna turned her head to look at the giant standing next to her bed. But the voice was human enough. This man was taller than her brother who was six feet. It couldn't be Rahul, of course. He wasn't as broad or muscular as this guy standing next to her. Rubbing her sleepy eyes, she got up to take a better look and heard him laugh. Oh my God! It *was* Rahul. He was grinning from ear to ear, all set to spray her with water once again.

"Rahul, you devil," shrieked Meghna as she catapulted into his arms, thrilled to bits when he caught her in a bear hug.

"Whoosh," Rahul pretended to become breathless when she threw herself into his arms. "I s'pose you must weigh a ton. You've grown up and how!" He exclaimed, holding her at arms' length, studying her all the way from the top of her tousled head to the tips of her bare toes.

Meghna's head used to barely reach his chest during those days. Now she was five feet eight inches tall with a slim figure and long, long legs. Rahul stared, fascinated. His eyes made a slow study of her, taking their time. "Wow!" The single syllable had more meaning to it than all the poetry in the world.

Her face turning crimson, Meghna moved away and rushed into speech to cover the unexpected feeling of shyness which overwhelmed her. "How're you? When did you come? How're your parents? I hope you'll be here for a while…" she fired away rapidly before stopping mid-sentence when he laughed out loud.

Rahul grinned at her; his brown eyes glowing. "Questions! Questions! I just came here directly from the airport. Reema *Bhabhi*'s preparing breakfast. You come along and let's talk at the dining table."

"Just give me a couple of minutes." Meghna rushed into the bathroom, brushed her teeth before washing and drying her face. Running a brush through her long silken dark brown hair, she stepped out.

Rahul was waiting for her in the room checking out the clutter on the work table next to the window.

"Same old Meghna. Messy desk," Rahul wrinkled his nose at her.

"I work comfortably the way it is," she responded defiantly.

"Typical," said Rahul.

"Rahul," Meghna raised her voice warningly.

Rahul put up both his hands, palms outward, "Peace," he grinned, his eyes teasing her.

"Peace, my foot," said Meghna, her eyes promising murder.

They walked into the hall where Reema was setting the table for breakfast.

"*Aloo parathas*, yummy! *Bhabhi*, you certainly know the way to a man's heart," Rahul gave Reema a wide smile as Sanjay pulled out a chair for his friend.

Reema returned his smile. The four of them sat down to a hot breakfast and aromatic tea flavoured with ginger.

"Mmm… heaven," smiled Rahul.

"And so, old man, what've you been doing with yourself, besides trying to impress your old cronies?" This was Sanjay.

"Just having fun. I've made a lot of friends. We go pub hopping at least a couple of nights in a week. I travel most of the long weekends. I've visited Paris, Berne and Oslo. Simply superb! You must be travelling a lot too, working for an international airline and all that. How come you never come to London?"

"I get to fly regular routes to some countries only. I'm hoping to travel to London beginning next year," said Sanjay.

"That's great. Please do bring *Bhabhi* and the kids along. Too bad if Meghna can't make it…"

Meghna threw a cloth napkin directly on Rahul's face.

"Ouch," he yelled, covering one eye and jumping to his feet.

"What happened, Rahul? Are you badly hurt? Meghna, how could you?" Reema was shocked.

Sanjay sat back calmly to watch the fun. He was transported to their student days when the three of them had argued, fought, and quarrelled over anything and everything under the sun.

Meghna felt contrite. She put a hand on Rahul's arm. "Rahul, I'm sorry. Does it hurt badly?"

Rahul removed the hand covering his right eye. It was obvious that he wasn't hurt one little bit.

"You pig, I should've known," grinned Meghna.

Rahul winked at her. He felt he was home after all these years. He had missed the easy camaraderie that existed between the three of them.

"Where are the kids?" asked Rahul, looking around.

"Still asleep and thank God for that. They don't wake up before nine," said Reema.

"So, Meghna, tell me, what've you been doing with yourself these past six years, besides growing up?" asked Rahul.

"Well, I've completed my BA. After that, I learnt various forms of western dance for a couple of years and now take dance classes for kids thrice a week. I also hold a job as copywriter at a website; the office is not far from here. And I read a lot." She shrugged her shoulders. "I've been on a few trips to Rajasthan, Himachal and Kerala. Nothing as hep as Europe," she grinned. She was happy for him. "I envy your overseas jaunts though," she smiled at him without a trace of jealousy in her voice. Her large grey eyes were intently studying the changes time had wrought on Rahul, her scrutiny bold.

He had been extremely tall and lanky before. Now he was broad and muscular. His biceps stood out prominently under the short sleeves of his t-shirt which stretched taut over the expanse of his wide chest.

Meghna extended a hand and touched his arm in wonder. "Rahul, what've you been doing to get this?" she asked.

"I went to a gym for a couple of years after I moved to England. I wanted to build some muscle into my lanky frame." His honey brown eyes twinkled with mirth. "Nowadays, I jog and swim alternately to keep fit. But that's enough about me. You seem to be doing a lot of things. I can understand that you dance. But teaching it? The poor tiny tots!" Rahul sighed dramatically. "The parents must be blind. If I remember right," he screwed up his face in concentration, "you had two left feet the only time we took you dancing. What a fiasco, eh, Sanjay!" He turned and looked at his friend, putting a hand up in high-five. Sanjay hit Rahul's palm with his and the two of them laughed long and loud until tears spilled from their eyes.

Meghna thought it was anything but amusing. She recalled the incident with all the anger and humiliation of a fifteen-year-old.

Reema had no clue as to what they were talking and laughing about. She looked from one to the other, her expression puzzled.

Rahul looked at her and said, "Let me explain, Reema *Bhabhi*. There was this party at a friend's…"

"Just shut up, Rahul. I'm sure *Bhabhi* will be bored to tears." Meghna's grey eyes spat venom.

"But…"

"Rahul, how could you? It has been barely a couple of hours since you came and you're already playing mischief," accused Meghna, her voice shaking with temper.

"Come on, Meghna, be a sport. It was too funny. You should be able to laugh it off after all these years, surely?" Sanjay interrupted in a calm voice, trying to pacify his sister.

Meghna refused to be calmed. She shuddered as the past unfolded in her mind's eye. She had been a very young fifteen and absolutely fascinated by the people swinging away to the pulsating music. Sanjay and Rahul dragged her into the small space set aside for dancers. It had been crowded to the hilt. Meghna panicked as strange bodies jostled against hers. The scene turned into a nightmare as she jumped first one way and then another, trying to dodge the sea of bodies. She stepped on many-a-toe in the process. Curses and epithets following her bungling progress, she finally hid herself in the bathroom until it was time to leave.

"It was anything but funny," insisted Meghna curtly before walking away. She could hear Reema scolding her husband in a hushed voice as she stepped into her bedroom.

A tear slowly found its way down her golden face as Meghna stood at the window. She dashed an angry hand against her cheek, only to have another one coming right after the first. The shock of meeting Rahul after so many years had taken its toll. Life had never been the same after Rahul kissed her that fateful day before he left for London. Meghna unconsciously touched her lips. All these years she had waited for him to contact her. And suddenly he was here, larger than life and—she clenched her fists—teasing her mercilessly. It appeared as if the years in between had ceased to exist. The tears flowed faster.

Rahul placed a gentle hand on her shoulder. "Meghna."

She tried to push his hand away, but in vain.

"Meghna, look at me." Rahul right hand came out to take hold of her chin and turned her head to face him.

There was no response as Meghna kept her gaze down, refusing to meet his teasing brown eyes.

"It's lovely. Your choice, I suppose," said Rahul.

Her head came up at that and she looked at him as if he had taken leave of his senses.

"The floor—the pattern's beautiful." Rahul explained patiently.

Meghna glared at him, confused.

"Where are your wits, my darling? Weren't you trying to draw my attention to the floor? I'm impressed. It looks great." His expression was serious even as his brown eyes danced.

"Rahul," said Meghna, "You're impossible, incorrigible and, and…"

"And?" prompted Rahul, his eyes alight with mischief.

Meghna just about managed to stop herself from saying, 'adorable'. The devil didn't need her to feed his already swollen ego. "And nothing."

"Nothing?" Rahul looked at the self-confident woman in front of him. He thought of the teenager—

short and plump with no confidence at all—he had left behind six years ago. His lips parted in a slow smile. "Why the tears?" He asked in a sudden change of subject.

Meghna had been watching the morning sun's rays playing on Rahul's handsome face, totally absorbed in the dashing figure he cut, and didn't hear his question.

"Meghna," Rahul's voice came from near her ear, curious at her wandering attention.

She raised startled grey eyes to his face which was too close for comfort. "What?"

"Why the tears?" he repeated.

"Forget it. It's nothing important," said Meghna.

"How can I? As you mentioned earlier, it's barely a few hours since…"

"Please Rahul. I'm perfectly fine." Meghna answered quickly, worried that he might leave.

"Would you rather I stayed elsewhere?" continued Rahul, "I don't want to upset you."

"Don't be silly, Rahul. Sanjay and *Bhabhi* will be very upset if you stayed elsewhere." Meghna refused to look above his shoulder.

"And you?" A dark eyebrow rose in query.

Afraid of saying the wrong thing, Meghna didn't reply. He had seemed like the Rahul from her childhood days in the dining room. Now he appeared to be a sophisticated stranger making demands on her that she didn't even begin to fathom. He was like an entirely new person. She didn't realise that the change was more in the way she perceived things; then as a teenager and now as a young woman.

Rahul snapped his fingers in front of Meghna's startled face, "Earth calling Meghna," he said, his face breaking into a wide grin.

Meghna brought her rambling thoughts under control and looked at him questioningly.

Rahul sighed extravagantly. "Meghna," he said, "Do you want me to leave?"

"Well," answered Meghna softly, "if you stay elsewhere, how will you find the opportunity to torment me?" She tried hard to look sad. But her twinkling eyes gave her away.

"That's my Meghna." Rahul put an arm around her shoulders. Thank God! For a minute there he had thought he was going to be thrown out of her home.

Meghna was just the perfect name for her. Her grey eyes reminded him of dark, rain-bearing clouds. The lightning temper in her eyes and the thunder in her expression added to his conviction. Just now the grey eyes were smiling guilelessly up at him.

The door suddenly opened and a pint-sized tornado hurled itself towards Meghna. "Aunty," squealed a childish voice.

Meghna slipped from under the muscular arm holding her and went down on her knees to greet her small niece, Sasha. "Good morning, sweetie pie," said Meghna as she gathered the bouncing body into her arms.

"Good Mornin', Aunty Me'na," the baby lisped before giving Meghna a loud, wet kiss on her cheek.

Rahul watched enviously as Meghna turned her other cheek to the child.

Meghna got up with her niece in her arms and turned around to introduce Rahul.

But Sasha had already recognised him. Thrusting out her chubby arms to him, "Unca Ra'ul, Unca Ra'ul," she chanted.

Rahul grinned at the baby as he took the excited bundle in his arms. He let out a sigh of pure joy as Sasha hugged him close, her plump arms wound tightly around his neck. Rahul laughed merrily as he pulled her closer and buried his nose in the small shoulder, inhaling the sweet baby smell. It was a mind riveting experience and completely novel to him.

Meghna turned as she heard the more sober, two-year-old Rehaan walk in. "Hi, sweetheart," she greeted her little nephew, bending down to kiss him.

He replied seriously, "Hi, Aunty." Being the extremely cautious young man he was, Rehaan didn't bother with her name as he couldn't pronounce it.

He stared solemnly at the tall stranger holding Sasha. "'Sha," he called out to his sister.

"Rehaan," shrieked Sasha from her high perch, "Unca Ra'ul," she introduced.

Rahul went down on his knees, gently letting go of Sasha. The little boy studied the stranger unblinkingly for a few moments before giving him a wide grin.

Meghna was astonished as Rehaan was not a friendly child, especially with strangers.

Rahul grinned back at Rehaan as the young man commanded in his baby voice, "Unca, lift Re'aan."

Rahul pulled him close and lifted him off the floor as Rehaan continued to tell him something. Though fascinated with the baby talk, Rahul looked at Meghna helplessly as he couldn't understand any of it.

"He wants you to sit with him at breakfast. Do feel honoured," interpreted Meghna.

"Oh!" Rahul turned to the little guy in his arms. "Sure, my friend, let's go."

Meghna watched Rahul leave her room with Rehaan in his arms and Sasha skipping along beside him, clinging to his hand trustingly.

A small sigh escaped her as Meghna turned around to have a shower and get ready for the day.

Rahul placed Rehaan on his high baby chair and turned to lift Sasha on to hers. He was fascinated by the little girl who looked like a miniature version of her aunt.

The serious Rehaan ate meticulously. The naughty Sasha dropped food all around and some of it landed on her nose. Rahul lifted a napkin and gently wiped the tiny, button nose while the child gurgled with pleasure.

Sanjay came out of his bedroom, dressed for work and the kids screamed for his attention. Dad was special as he was away so often. Sanjay grabbed the apron his wife was wearing and hurriedly tied it around his suit to save it from grubby hands. Rahul watched enviously as the kids bonded with their father.

"You need a suit of armour rather than that apron." Rahul smiled at his friend.

"I know," grimaced Sanjay as he gently untangled his tie from the death grip Rehaan had on it, ruffling his son's hair affectionately.

"Daddy has to go to office," he explained patiently to the two-year-old. "We'll go swimming in the evening."

"Simming, simming," chorused the children as Sasha banged the spoon rhythmically against her empty milk mug.

Sanjay spoke to Rahul, "I'll see you in the evening, *yaar*. I need to fly today but will take a few days off from tomorrow."

"Just chill, Sanjay, I'm okay. I'll take the kids down to the garden I saw on my way up, if it's alright with you, *Bhabhi*," he said, looking at Reema.

The children's heads cocked up as they realised that Rahul was talking about them and made the right connection with the word 'garden'.

"Unca Ra'ul, garden," they went on and on.

Reema looked at their guest in mock amazement and said, "Are you sure? Neither my kids nor I will let you go without holding you to that promise," she laughed.

Meghna walked in all dressed up and ready for her dance classes. She wore a leotard which fit her like a second skin and a sleeveless, hip-length leather jacket.

She took a cloth napkin, wet it under the sink and walked purposely to her niece and nephew. Rehaan submitted quietly as she wiped his mouth and hands.

Sasha protested long and loud as if she was being slaughtered. Rahul took the napkin from Meghna's hand.

"Sasha," the child looked up, rebellion in the large grey eyes that so reminded him of her aunt. He handed the napkin to her. Reema had already removed the plate, mug and spoon out of harm's way. "Come on darling, let's show everyone how well you can wipe your hands and face." Sasha rose to the challenge beautifully and wiped her face and hands carefully and neatly. "Good girl," the compliment brought a smile of delight to the cherub's face.

Meghna turned around to say 'bye' to everyone.

Rahul caught her eye and grinned broadly. "How do you commute to work, Meghna?" asked Rahul.

"On my motorbike," answered Meghna.

"What?" Rahul was startled to say the least. He turned to look at Sanjay for confirmation.

Sanjay stood grinning as he nodded.

"Is that safe?" Rahul looked from Sanjay to Meghna and back again.

"Why not?" Meghna was quick to the defence, her voice angry.

"Well, you know how the traffic is, and…"

"You mean you'd ne'er ride a bike on the Mumbai roads?" Meghna asked sarcastically.

"I'm different, Meghna. You…"

Meghna didn't let him finish what he was going to say. Her eyes blazed like thunder as she walked up to Rahul and stood in front of him, her hands on her hips. She suddenly poked a finger at his chest and said, "You male chauvinist pig! In what way is it different?"

"Well," Rahul pretended to consider her question seriously. "A bike's quite heavy for a lady, Meghna." He turned to Sanjay for support.

Sanjay saw the genuine concern on his friend's face and said, "Rahul, I don't think you should worry.

Meghna's an expert. Do you think I'd let her ride a bike otherwise?"

Rahul was finally convinced by Sanjay's words. He turned to Meghna with mischief dancing in his eyes, "This I must see."

"Get lost," Meghna flounced away in anger and catching hold of Sanjay's arm, pulled him towards the doorway. "Let's go, Sanjay."

Sanjay lifted his hand in farewell to his family and Rahul before walking to the lift with his younger sister.

On their way down, Sanjay put his arm around Meghna and asked her, "Happy?" He knew Meghna was deeply attracted to Rahul.

Meghna raised sparkling eyes to her brother's face. "Yep," she said in a cheerful voice.

"Why don't you also take a few days off, Meghna?" asked Sanjay.

"Let me see, the office should be fine, but the dance classes," she shrugged, "I'll check."

"You do that." They had reached the basement where Sanjay moved to his Toyota Fortuner and Meghna to her Hero Honda.

5

Meghna tried her best to control herself from grinning ear-to-ear on her way to the dance classes near Five Gardens at Dadar. She was glad that no one could see her expression thanks to her helmet.

What a wonderful surprise to be woken up by Rahul this morning. Cheeky Devil! He hadn't changed one little bit—always one for pranks and practical jokes, mischief gleaming out of his eyes during all waking hours. He had dragged the sober Sanjay into many-a-scrape in those days. Sushma had never had the heart to scold him despite all the complaints she received. People never spoke to his mother, Rajni, about Rahul. Shyam Sinha was always busy travelling on business and had felt relieved at Rahul finding a surrogate mother in Sushma.

Meghna sighed with pleasure. Rahul was back. All the years of waiting was finally at an end. She couldn't really remember when she fell in love with him. It had been gradual as she became an adult.

She reached the Parsi Club with ten minutes to spare before the class. Prashant was waiting for her inside the compound as usual. Meghna removed her helmet to give him an extra wide smile.

"Good morning, Prashant."

"Morning, Meghna!" Prashant taught at the dance classes along with her. They had met during a dance show on TV they had taken part in. While both were above average, neither had won an award. They had hit it off from the first round and had decided to open their own dance classes. The Parsi Club at Dadar was ideal as she lived in Sion and he stayed in Wadala.

Meghna saw the curiosity in his eyes and realised that she was grinning way too much. Without saying anything, she tucked her arm in his and walked towards the classroom.

They went to the main hall where the sessions were held. Their students ranged from age three to ten. There were twenty in all for the class from ten to eleven in the morning—thrice a week. The other three days there was another batch of twenty. The class number stood at twenty only because Prashant and Meghna refused to take more.

Then there was the batch between 11.30 and 12.30, the age group being eleven to sixteen. Meghna loved teaching dance and had an excellent rapport with her students. She and Prashant had been running these classes for two years. Meghna believed that dancing was a wonderful way to keep one's mind and body fit. Even Sunday found her swinging away to music with her nephew and niece.

Prashant lusted after Meghna and hoped to take her out. But his attempts to date her had all been in vain. She simply refused to meet him socially.

They waited for all the students to assemble before starting the class on time. Soft music played from the speakers, a mixture of both Hindi and English pop songs as Meghna started out with simple steps in front of the enthusiastic kids. Prashant walked among them correcting a child's step here and another there.

The hour passed by like a dream as Meghna danced along, only half her attention on them as her thoughts kept going back to Rahul, a small secret smile never far away from her lips.

A bell pealed, signalling the end of the hour and the kids packed up and left with obvious reluctance. Meghna walked over gracefully to the bathroom to wipe away the sweat with a wet wipe. She looked at herself in the mirror. A grin broke out on her face which appeared more alive than usual. Tendrils of hair escaped from her top knot and seemed to have a life of their own, dancing to some silent tune as if in celebration.

"Rahul!" Meghna mouthed his name without sound. Her body vibrated in delicious excitement. She would have to wait until she reached her office to share it with someone. Sarika was her best friend and the two of them worked for a commercial website. They were of the same age and shared each other's deepest secrets.

She went back to the hall where Prashant waited with a cup of coffee. "Thanks, Prashant," she said before lifting the cup to her lips. She was in no mood for a chat and Prashant gave up after a couple of attempts.

The next batch began to arrive and Meghna was thrilled to get back to her favourite profession. The older set was even more fun as they were much more graceful and appreciative.

It was 12.45 when Meghna left the club. She went back home for a bite of lunch. She let herself into the flat, looking forward to sparring words with Rahul once again.

The place was quiet, before Reema called out from the kitchen, "Is that you, Meghna?"

"Yes, *Bhabhi*. Where's everyone?" Meghna walked into the kitchen as Reema was putting the finishing touches to the meal.

"They're down in the garden. Although I adore the brats, sometimes, you know, it's a relief to be on my own." Reema smiled.

"I know, *Bhabhi*. You work too hard." She hugged Reema. "You've been wonderful to Sanjay and me."

"Flattery will get you everywhere, my dear," Reema teased.

The two of them brought all the hot cases containing the various dishes to the dining table. "*Bhabhi*, you've gone to a lot of trouble."

"But of course. Rahul loves to eat, especially Indian food and you know I enjoy cooking," replied Reema.

Meghna went to her room to change out of her leotard into a pair of jeans and a semi-formal shirt. She then sat at the table to taste a little bit of everything. Reema sat with her, keeping her company while sipping her mid-morning tea.

"How do you feel now that your dream hero has turned up?" asked Reema.

Meghna raised startled grey eyes to her sister-in-law. Reema was grinning at her, her eyebrows lifted in query. Meghna looked down, her face going red.

"*Bhabhi*," she was hesitant, "Is it so obvious?"

"Only to me and Sanjay," laughed Reema.

"Phew! For a minute there I thought the whole world must know." Her worry was that maybe Rahul knew too.

"And what do you plan to do now he's here?"

"Why, nothing *Bhabhi*. I'm not even sure I know this new Rahul." Meghna's lips drooped at the corners.

The doorbell rang and Meghna's heart bounced up into her throat.

It was Rahul and the kids, dirty from their romp in the garden. "Hey," he called out to Meghna, his eyes studying her keenly. "How was your morning?"

Neither of them noticed when Reema took the children to their room for a bath.

"Lovely, thanks." Her answering smile was a tad nervous, not quite reaching her eyes. "You've obviously been enjoying yourself with Sasha and Rehaan in the garden."

"Yes." Rahul's eyes twinkled. "They're adorable. I've not had such fun in a long time." He was also filthy with grass stains over his shorts and t-shirt. He intercepted Meghna's look and grimaced, "Yeah, I know I need a shower." He turned in the direction of the guest bedroom.

"Let me say 'bye' then. I'm leaving for work."

"Oh!" Was there a trace of disappointment in his voice as he uttered that single syllable? It was hard to say. "I thought you'd taken the afternoon off."

"I've to go. See you later." Meghna left the flat without turning to look at him. She met Sarika at the gate to their office. The two of them rushed up to the second floor where their office was situated.

The moment they sat down, Sarika spoke, "Come on, out with it. What's up? Tell me now."

Meghna gave her a broad grin before saying, "You'd never guess what happened."

"NOW Meghna, before I die of curiosity," the bubbly Sarika insisted.

"Rahul has come," said Meghna in a stage whisper while turning around to switch on her computer.

"What?" shrieked Sarika, dropping the papers she was feeding into the printer. "Your Rahul?" she asked as she bent down to pick the scattered papers.

"The one and only," Meghna answered with glee.

"And? Tell me what happened, fast," Sarika insisted.

"And nothing." Meghna's voice was anything but calm.

"What do you mean nothing? Come on, Meghna, you can tell me," Sarika pouted at her friend.

Meghna smiled. "Really, Sarika. There's nothing much to say. He seems all grown up and different. I don't quite know myself what's happening."

"You mean you don't feel the spark and sizzle any longer?" Sarika was disappointed.

"No, no," Meghna eyes were dreamy. "Of course, I felt the thrill and excitement, immediately. He looks gorgeous, you know. Better than before. He's big and muscular and so handsome." Her voice turned uncertain. "Do you think he'd be interested in simple old me? He must've met such lovely girls in London." She appeared wistful as she uttered those words.

Sarika snapped her fingers in front of Meghna's face. "Meghna, you're a beauty yourself," she said loyally. "And Rahul, I presume, is still single. Don't expect trouble where there's none," she insisted.

After that, silence reigned as the two of them concentrated on their work. The girls worked very hard and sincerely. Their boss, Akash Mehra, usually came in at about four in the evening. When Meghna asked him for ten days' leave, he agreed to it immediately as she had a couple of months' leave accumulated.

It was late evening. Sanjay and Reema had taken their kids down to the club house in the building compound.

Meghna sat in front of the television pressing the buttons on the remote disinterestedly. There was nothing to hold her attention. She was restless, waiting for Rahul who was sleeping off his jet lag.

She had changed into a short skirt and sleeveless top after returning from work. She had been so looking forward to sparring words with Rahul only to find that he was fast asleep. She was tempted to go into his room and wake him up rudely, the way he had woken her up that morning. The thought brought a smile to Meghna's face. But she didn't have the confidence to walk into his bedroom.

She kept looking at the wall clock every few seconds. She let out an unconscious sigh as she felt that the lazy hands of the clock appeared to be slower than ever.

"What was that for?" asked Rahul from the doorway to the guest bedroom.

Meghna jumped and the remote flew out of her hands to land with a light thud on the nearby sofa. She turned startled eyes to Rahul.

He was standing there wearing only a pair of cotton corduroy pants. *Damn him*, thought Meghna, as he smiled cheekily at her. Meghna smiled vaguely in his direction, refusing to meet his eyes. And shyness gripped her in its hold as she couldn't help stealing brief glances at the expanse of his naked chest.

"Hey!" called out Rahul.

"Hi!" whispered Meghna in reply, staring blindly at the TV.

"Where's everyone?" the voice moved closer.

Panic rose in Meghna's throat, almost choking her. "They've gone swimming. Let me get you some coffee." She moved fast, making her escape to the kitchen. Her hands shook as she assembled a tray with coffee mugs and sugar. She lit the gas stove to heat the milk. She had not heard Rahul following her, his bare feet making no noise.

He reached out with a long arm to switch off the stove. His other arm came from around her left side to encircle her in a loose embrace. Rahul didn't utter a word; his heavy breath the only indication of his reaction to her proximity.

Meghna stood stiffly in the circle of his arms, waiting, both petrified and excited, for his next move. She turned her head to the left and looked at him from under her eyelashes.

He turned her around to pull her close to his bare chest and pressed his lips to her flaming cheek, before pushing the hair away from her neck and exploring her sensitive nape with his lips.

She made a slight sound of protest before burying her hot face in his shoulder, slipping her arms around his waist even as a soft sigh escaped her.

"Meghna." He sounded serious for once. He pulled her face up to his, a large hand in her hair.

But her lovely grey eyes would look anywhere but at him.

"Meghna," Rahul bent down to kiss her full on her mouth.

Her startled lips and eyes opened wide. Her eyelids slowly came down as he gently moved his mouth back and forth over hers.

He raised his head to look at her face once again. "It has been so long," he whispered, pressing his forehead to hers.

"Mmm…" Meghna's throat was dry. Her hands moved slowly on his chest, her palms tingling from the contact; continuing to keep her eyes closed.

Rahul stopped her foraging hands with his and drew a finger down her cheek, smiling when she finally opened her eyes.

She suddenly realised what was happening and removed her hands from his chest in a hurry as if stung. She extricated herself from his arms and turned her back to him and muttered something about making coffee.

He gave her an indulgent smile before saying, "You do that. I'll get some clothes on," and walked towards his room, whistling tunelessly.

Meghna felt completely shaken by Rahul's kiss. It was nothing like the innocent one he had bestowed on her six years ago. She glared at his back and muttered, "Idiot."

"I heard that," called back his cheery voice, grinning devilishly when she made a face at him. "Cute," he blew her a kiss before disappearing into his bedroom.

Meghna laid out the coffee tray in the hall and waited for 'His Highness' to appear.

Rahul was back in a few minutes and seated himself very close to her before picking up a coffee cup. She tried to inch away slowly, only his hand shot out to hold her still.

"You're not having any coffee?" asked Rahul, his brown eyes studying her face intently.

Meghna picked up her cup with shaking hands and lifted it to her lips. She couldn't meet the molten honey of his gaze, not to save her life. *At least he was keeping his hands to himself now,* she thought, breathing easier.

They finished their coffee in silence. Rahul got up, took the tray to the kitchen and rinsed the cups at the sink, leaving them on the draining board, gaining Meghna some precious moments to calm down.

She refused to look at Rahul or utter a word as they left the flat. They were alone in the lift on their way down. Rahul stood a good two feet away from her. "You look gorgeous," he said, his voice soft, eyeing her long, slender legs exposed by the short skirt.

She looked up with a smile to see his eyes twinkling. He put an arm around her shoulders and pulled her close in a friendly hug.

The children were having a gala time in the swimming pool. Even the quiet Rehaan's face was animated. He was riding piggy back on his father as Sanjay swam from one end of the pool to the other. Sasha was showing off her diving prowess to anyone who was interested.

"Unca Ra'ul, Aunty Me'na," yelled Sasha, "watch me dive." Rahul and Meghna moved to the end where the diving boards were.

'One, two, thee," lisped Sasha before making a clean dive. She was an excellent swimmer. Both her aunt and uncle clapped loudly in appreciation as her head bobbed out of the water. She waved to them in response, rubbing the water from her eyes.

Rehaan wanted to show off too. He swam well but was no good at diving. He jumped out of the pool and ran to the diving board in a flash. Reema's warning voice came too late. He had already jumped into the deep end and Meghna's breath caught in her chest as she waited for his tiny head to bob up. Her heart was in her throat in the half minute it took Sanjay to get his spluttering son out of the deep end. It became obvious that it was Rehaan's self-esteem that was hurt more than his person as the little boy buried his face against his father's shoulder and refused to look at anyone.

"Rehaan," called out Reema, holding her arms out to her son. She was visibly shaken. Rehaan jumped into her arms, almost knocking the two of them over, Sanjay just managing to hold his wife afloat. Rehaan looked at his mother's face and his tiny, defiant face crumpled into tears. He tucked his thumb into his mouth and his face against his mother.

"Come on folks, time to go," called out Sanjay in a loud voice.

His daughter's face turned mutinous. "I want to s'im some more," she declared loudly.

Reema felt sorry for her daughter. Her moment of glory had been short lived. She nudged her husband gently and shook her head.

Meghna brought a dry towel and called out, "Rehaan, sweetheart, come to Aunty Meghna. I'll cuddle you and squash you and…"

He giggled and put his arms out to her. She lifted him and wrapped him in the towel before taking him away. Meghna made a 'thumbs up' sign to the rest of the family to go ahead with the diving session; before she and Rehaan chattered their way to the changing room.

Rahul felt torn as he watched Meghna's swinging hips moving away from him. He was keen to follow the duo but it was obvious that Sasha wanted him to admire her diving skills. He smiled at the little girl encouragingly, "Come on Sasha; let me see that fabulous dive again."

Sasha was thrilled to be the centre of attention once again and rushed to the diving board. Sanjay let her have her own way a few more times before calling a halt. "Come baby, it's time for dinner."

A protesting Sasha came out of the pool with great reluctance. Rahul wrapped a towel around her shivering body and pulled her close. "That was fantastic, Sasha. You're an amazing swimmer."

Sasha lapped up the compliment and gave Rahul a loud kiss. "You should also come tomorrow, Unca Ra'ul."

"Sure, sweetheart."

"Not tomorrow, sweetie," said Sanjay. He was very careful with the promises he made to his kids.

Sasha screwed up her little face to glare at her father. "Why Daddy?" she demanded to know.

"Because we're going to the *Dandiya Raas*. It's *Navratri* from tomorrow," answered Sanjay, ruffling his daughter's hair after pulling off the bright red swimming cap that matched her one-piece swimming suit.

Rahul liked the way Sanjay treated his daughter, like an adult. The young lady laughed at her father and clapped her hands before wrapping her arms tightly around his dripping legs.

"Don't, sweetie, you'll get wet again," Sanjay lifted Sasha off the ground to plant a kiss on her nose as she giggled at him.

Reema separated her protesting daughter from her father and took off towards the changing room.

"So Rahul, did you sleep off your jet lag?" Sanjay asked his closest friend.

Rahul sighed even as he nodded. "*Arre yaar*, Sanjay, I envy you. You've a wonderful family," he said, clapping Sanjay on his shoulder.

Sanjay smiled at Rahul. "And what's stopping you from having one of your own?"

Rahul shrugged his shoulders. "It's a big commitment, *yaar*. It scares me to think of being tied to someone for life."

"The sacrifice, if you want to call it one, is definitely worth it." It was Sanjay's voice of experience.

"You've been lucky in getting Reema *Bhabhi*. She's great." Rahul was envious.

Sanjay's teeth flashed white on his golden face. "Oh, I very much appreciate her. Especially," his eyes turned sad, "since Mamma passed away. She has been a tower of strength. I couldn't have managed Meghna on my own. She was inconsolable for months together."

Rahul's face darkened on hearing Sanjay's words. He realised guiltily that he had partly been responsible for Meghna's sorrow.

The woman lingering in his thoughts walked back with Rehaan in tow. "Why don't you guys wait in the lounge? I'll be back in ten." Sanjay moved towards the changing rooms, ruffling his son's dark head on his way. Child-like, Rehaan had forgotten his embarrassment and gave Rahul a dazzling smile.

Rahul lifted Rehaan in his arms and threw him up in the air before catching him. Rehaan gurgled with laughter as they made their way slowly to the lounge.

Rahul turned to Meghna, "What would you like to drink?"

"'Epsi," piped Rehaan as Meghna shook her head.

"Nothing for me, thank you," she replied formally.

Rahul looked at her while she refused to meet his gaze. He shrugged his broad shoulders and turned to his best friend's son. "One Pepsi coming up for Rehaan," he declared, tickling the child who giggled helplessly.

He placed him on a chair beside Meghna before walking to the bar to get their drinks.

Meghna's eyes followed his progress. It was easier without his knowing eyes watching her every move. Rahul suddenly turned to catch her gaze on him and dropped one eyelid in a wink, bringing hot colour to her face.

Reema and Sanjay walked in at that moment with Sasha skipping along between them. She looked adorable in a pair of hot pink shorts and a matching t-shirt. She ran up to Rahul and caught hold of his trouser leg.

"Unca Ra'ul, Pepsi," she told him clearly.

"Sure, sweetie," said Rahul. "Why don't you go sit with Meghna Aunty and Rehaan like a good girl? I'll get the drinks in a minute."

"Okay," Sasha agreed before going to sit at the table.

Sanjay pulled out a chair for Reema before joining Rahul at the bar.

Reema sat next to her sister-in-law, moving the water glass out of Rehaan's reach. She was constantly on alert mode with her children around.

Dinner was a noisy affair. It was 10.30 by the time they finished and Rehaan's eyelids were drooping by now.

They got up to leave when Rahul placed a hand on Meghna's arm. "Let's go for a walk." His eyes challenged her to refuse him.

She eyed him warily as one would a stalking tiger.

Sanjay had walked ahead with Rehaan in his arms when he realised that the other two were not with them. A smile tugged at one corner of his mouth when he turned around to see his sister and best friend walking in the opposite direction.

Rahul enfolded Meghna's hand in his large one before stepping towards the main gate.

"Where do you want to go?" she asked.

"Nowhere special, just getting the feel of this place. It has been so long." He smiled down at her. Not seeing an answering smile on her face, he asked, "Is something bothering you?"

Meghna almost said, 'You' before saying, "Nothing."

"Why the murderous expression? Have I done something that you don't approve of?" His smile turned roguish, his eyes lighting up with devilry. "The kiss not good enough for the sophisticated Meghna?" he asked, tongue firmly tucked in cheek.

Meghna's grey eyes turned thunderous. "Rahul," she snarled, "Can we talk about something else?"

"Hmm… like how sexy you look?" His voice had become a soft rumble in her ear as he stepped closer. "How your grey eyes flash like lightening when you're in a temper, which you're in most of the time." His smile widened, "Or what gorgeous…"

Meghna stopped abruptly and pressed her hand against Rahul's mouth. "Stop it, Rahul," she commanded, her eyes spitting fire at him.

He caught her wrist to hold her hand against his mouth and kissed her fingers, the mischief not leaving his eyes.

"I give up." Meghna tried to pull her hand in vain. "Let me go, Rahul."

"Say please," said Rahul, his voice gentle.

"Why the hell should I say please? It's my hand. Just let go."

"And let you attack me again? No way." Laughter laced his words.

"What?" squealed Meghna, "Attack you? Are you crazy! Will you let go of me?" She refused to look at him.

"Meghna!" She turned her head away. "Okay, if that's the way it is, let's go." Rahul shrugged his shoulders before walking ahead, her hand held firmly to his lips, forcing her to fall in step with him.

"Rahul, this is ridiculous." Meghna stamped her foot, not very successfully, not with her arm held fast by her tormentor, her hand pressed to his mouth.

He stopped in his tracks. "What's ridiculous?" he asked, an innocent expression on his rugged face.

"You holding my hand like this." She pulled hard, trying to extract herself from his grip. Only he wouldn't budge. "Let go."

"Please," said Rahul, his eyes compelling her to say it.

She gave him another glare before turning her head away, saying, "Please."

"What was that? I didn't quite catch what you said." He almost exploded with mirth, enjoying riling her. She rose to his bait, every time.

"Rahul," her voice trembled with fury.

"Okay, okay," he let her go finally only to have her turn on him, both her hands clenched into tight fists, raining hard blows on his chest.

"Ouch, stop that, Meghna. I said *stop it*," growled Rahul, holding her by her arms.

But the blows continued to fall. "Say *please*," she said, looking at him in triumph.

"*Touché*," he grinned before saying in a pleading voice, "Please Meghna honey, stop beating me up." His voice dropped to a whisper, "Good enough?"

Meghna stopped hitting him abruptly, hearing his fake plea. Her heartbeat soared, sounding like a drum roll when she heard him call her 'honey' in that soft, sexy voice of his. She looked at Rahul as he held her tight fists against his chest.

"Meghna," He pulled her to the side of the path and leaned against a large tree trunk, keeping a loose hold on her. "What do you say we go jogging in the early morning?" asked Rahul, watching her intently.

"And cool off at the swimming pool soon after. That would be lovely. Shall we go up to the Fort Hill Garden?"

"Are you sure? That place is too messy for a comfortable walk, let alone jogging or running."

"Not recently, no. It's all spruced up, way cleaner and greener than before. Why don't you find out for yourself? Shall we leave at 6.30 am or is that too early for you?"

Rahul shrugged. "Then I suppose I'd better let you get your beauty's sleep." The teasing smile that had not been very far, lit up Rahul's face.

Meghna was curious to know how long he planned to be in Mumbai. She asked, "What are you plans?"

A puzzled frown appeared on Rahul's face. "You heard me. We'll go for a walk and swim in the morning."

"No, not that. How long do you plan to be in Mumbai?"

"Oh!" Rahul's brow cleared. "You want to know when I'm leaving for London."

Meghna darted a killing look at him. Jerking her arm from his loose grip, she started walking towards home. "Idiot," she muttered to herself. "Impossible, incorrigible, unreasonable moron! Just my luck to fall for a guy like him." She continued to mutter in a frustrated voice as Rahul caught up with her. He stopped her mid-stride and turned her to face him. She scowled at him, her lips pursed mutinously, her eyes like stormy clouds.

Rahul stared in fascination. She was beautiful. Temper added lustre to her face and he couldn't have looked away even if he wanted to. This must be the reason why he baited her all the time.

"Hmm…" he looked at her thoughtfully, "Now I know where Sasha gets her stubborn streak from. I did wonder as I believe both Sanjay and Reema *Bhabhi* have a mild temper and Sushma Aunty…" he counted on his fingers one by one.

Meghna slapped his counting hand and snarled, "Enough. Do you hear me? Enough." She was in a boiling rage. "You're right. I did want to know when you were leaving, so that I could continue to live my life in peace." Her chest heaved as she tried to control the urge to beat him on his chest again, her fists clenched against the soft cotton of his shirt. But something in his expression told her that he was waiting for her to do just that.

Rahul was enjoying himself too much. Meghna looked too beautiful for words and she was beside herself in anger to notice his eyes devouring her. He had a strong urge to drag her into his arms and kiss her senseless. All that passion and temper, wow! But somehow, he didn't think she would appreciate that just now. He decided to bide his time.

"Meghna," he spoke in a soothing voice, as though he was talking to a wild animal he was trying to tame.

Meghna looked at him warily. "What now?"

"Listen to me, will you? I'm sure you're tired after a long day. Why don't we continue this conversation tomorrow?"

Frustrated tears found their way down Meghna's cheeks. She turned away in disgust. *Oh, what was the use?* she thought to herself. She will never get to know what Rahul was thinking, not in a hundred years. A sob tore at her throat, seeking release. For an instant, she pictured herself becoming an old maid, waiting for him in vain while he laughed his way through life. The tears flowed faster.

"Meghna." A gentle arm encircled her shaking shoulders while the other arm came around to hold her in a close embrace. Rahul pushed her head into his broad shoulder and looked at the dark brown head in confusion. What should he do? His feelings for Meghna were powerful, in fact the strongest he had felt towards any woman. But still, was that enough for a lifelong commitment?

He thought of his parents. His poor father! Rahul felt so sorry for him. It was not as if he thought that Meghna was like his mother Rajni. But what about his own basic nature? His mother's blood ran in Rahul's veins. What if he made an awful spouse? The thought had kept him awake on many-a-night.

All those nights when he had lain awake, wondering whether Meghna had found another man, if she had fallen in love with someone else. He had waited all these years, giving her a chance to grow up, to meet other people, ensuring that he never spoke to her nor enquired about her.

But—he mentally shrugged his shoulders—there was a limit to a man's patience. He had felt a desperate need to see Meghna for himself, find out what she had become and whether she was interested in someone else.

And now, he was here with the girl of his dreams in his arms. She had grown up to be much more than his expectations, more beautiful, more graceful and sexier than any other woman he had met. Rahul's lips curled in a smile. And he, the jerk that he was, was making her lose her temper all the time.

"Meghna," Rahul stroked her hair gently. "Calm down, honey. I've three weeks' leave and I want to spend the time with you, getting to know you, the new grown-up Meghna." There, it was out, the actual reason for his trip to his hometown in India.

Meghna raised her face to look at him with tear-drenched eyes, hope beginning to dawn amidst the grey clouds. "Really?"

"Yeah, really." Rahul turned his gaze away from hers, reluctantly removed his arms from around her and moved away a couple of inches. "Look here, Meghna. I don't want to make promises. I'm scared of commitment, to be truthful. But I feel this frightful urge, need, call it whatever, to get to know you better." He puckered his brows as he thought of the right words to express his feelings. "You're so different from the adolescent I left behind. I've given you enough time and more to find yourself a partner. Since you haven't found anyone…"

"How do you know?" asked Meghna, fixing her grey eyes on his face, watching out for every single nuance in his expression.

Rahul jerked his head in her direction and stared at her for a few seconds, his brown gaze intense. A slow, satisfied smile spread on his face as he watched the colour rush up her cheeks. "I'm sure you wouldn't kiss me the way you do if you're interested in someone else."

She had no reply to this.

"So, my Meghna, do bear with me for a few weeks. I want to spend as much time with you as possible. We can get to know each other and," he shrugged his shoulders, "let's take it from there."

Meghna thought about what he said. It sounded reasonable enough. She needed time too, without any commitment. This man in front of her, this stranger, was quite different from the Rahul she knew from her childhood. She agreed that it made sense to wait.

She gave Rahul a small nod of agreement and put her hand trustingly in his large one when he thrust it out.

"Right," he pulled her into his arms, "let's seal the pact," and proceeded to kiss her thoroughly. Meghna linked her arms around his neck and stood on tiptoe to give better access to his marauding lips and hands. She sighed with pleasure as he plundered the depths of her mouth, seeking to quench his thirst, an undying craving he had acquired from the day he kissed the sixteen-year-old some years ago, a longing only this woman seemed to have the power to assuage. He buried his face against her soft, scented neck, his body shuddering with passion, trying hard to bring himself under control. It was a good thing there weren't too many people passing by at that time of the night, not that it seemed to bother the couple on the threshold of rediscovering each other.

"Is this a part of the getting-to-know-each-other process?" asked Meghna in a soft voice.

Rahul stared at her in wonder. Was this the same woman with the stormy, tear-drenched eyes? A gentle, teasing light shone from her eyes, her cheeks flushed with excitement, her slightly parted lips swollen pink from his kisses.

He recovered from his trance to reply, "Yeah, why not?"

"But Rahul, is it fair?"

Rahul placed the tip of his index finger on her mouth, inadvertently tracing the shape of her lips, shook his head, and said, "Don't deny me this. I'll go crazy not touching you, kissing you. Please Meghna. I'll not hurt you, I promise," he pleaded roughly, not used to requesting things, always having had his own way.

Meghna looked at him with a smile on her face. She thought to herself, *what difference will the next few weeks make to my feelings?* None, unless she fell more deeply in love with this handsome hunk. Alternately, there was a chance that he might fall in love with her. The hugs and kisses were a bonus. Why miss out on them? Probably the memories will be her only companion in the years to come if Rahul went away, leaving her.

Meghna shook herself out of her stupor. What had come over her? She would be crazy to allow him to kiss her whenever he pleased. That would be madness. And what would happen if and when he upped and left three weeks later? Would she ever recover from the loss? She shuddered at the thought. Her features hardened as she reached a firm decision.

"No."

"No?" Rahul scowled, not sure that he heard her right.

"No, Rahul. I don't want you to touch me and kiss me whenever it suits you. Let's get to know each other by all means. But *hands off*!" Meghna didn't mince her words.

"Meghna, don't be silly. Didn't I tell you that I'll not hurt you in any way?"

Meghna gave him a bitter smile. He obviously didn't understand how a woman's mind worked. "No, Rahul."

"Now who's being unreasonable? What's the harm in a few kisses? And they give us such joy too. Don't you dare deny it." Rahul was losing his cool, slowly but surely.

"Well, you heard me. There isn't much else to discuss. I agreed with you when you said that we should get to know each other. Why can't you respect my wishes?"

"But, Meghna," Rahul's voice switched from anger to persuasion in the matter of seconds, "be reasonable, honey. Please…"

Meghna dug her heels in and poked a finger at his chest, "You listen to me. Either you agree to keep your hands to yourself or the whole deal's off."

Rahul studied her face for a few seconds in silence, trying to find any kind of softening in her expression. Finding none, he said with a complete lack of enthusiasm, "You haven't left me with a choice," the irritation obvious in his voice.

A small triumphant smile formed on Meghna's face as she replied, "Smart of you to notice."

Rahul glared at her before continuing to walk towards home. Meghna fell into step beside him before asking, her voice sweetly innocent, "Are you sulking, by any chance?" She just managed to hold back her mirth.

Rahul turned around and fixed his brown eyes on her. They were glowing with temper, the colour of molten honey. "I don't sulk," he told her clearly.

"Okay then, my mistake," agreed Meghna cheerfully, tucking her arm into his.

eghna was up at six in the morning and got dressed in a pair of denim shorts, a red t-shirt and sneakers. She wore her swim suit under her clothes and carried a large bath towel in a beach bag.

She made coffee and waited for Rahul to appear. It was twenty minutes past six and still no sound from behind his door. She knocked a couple of times and when there was no response, opened the door a few inches to peep inside.

Rahul was lying sprawled across the bed on his front, with the covers askew. Meghna moved towards the bed for a closer look at the angelic face with the mocking eyes closed in sleep. His lips were parted slightly. A lock of dark hair that had fallen on his forehead made her hands itch to push it back in place. He looked so big and handsome and at peace, his long lashes resting against his hard cheeks, his breath coming out evenly. His exposed back was tanned to an even brown, hard muscles rippling under his skin. Meghna stared at his sleeping form, fascinated, her hands clasped tightly together to control the urge to touch him.

She moved closer and called out, "Rahul."

There was no change in the rhythm of his breathing. After calling out a couple of more times, Meghna placed a hand on his smooth shoulder and shook him awake, her fingers automatically curling around his shoulder in a caress as she whispered, "Rahul," once again.

"Good morning."

Meghna started guiltily as she found a pair of honey brown eyes gazing at her steadily. She removed her hand from his shoulder abruptly, colour spreading on her cheeks when he said, "The hands-off warning applies to me only, I s'pose."

She refused to rise to the bait as she replied, "Good morning, Rahul. It's time to leave." She looked at a point beyond his shoulders, not daring to meet his eyes.

Rahul looked at his watch that lay on the side table and said, "Oops, we're running late. Just give me a few minutes, honey." Meghna fled the moment he placed his bare legs on the floor.

Rahul gulped down the coffee Meghna offered him before leaving the flat carrying a backpack. They kept their bags in a locker at the club house and left the compound by the back gate.

Rahul looked around curiously, noting the various changes that had taken place in the area during his absence. They reached the Jawaharlal Nehru Hill Garden within a few minutes and entered the gates to climb up the steps.

The moment they reached the upper level, he could see the difference. The whole place looked so green and refreshing in the morning light. The eastern sky was alight although the rising sun itself was not yet visible from their vantage point. Rahul automatically took Meghna's hand as they turned left to make a clockwise round of the hill, sticking to the path.

Rahul was unusually quiet. He hadn't uttered a single word since they left the flat, in fact. Meghna kept watching him from the corner of her eyes. Although she had told him very strictly to keep his hands off, one small part of her mind lived in the hope that Rahul being what he was, wouldn't take her too seriously. She had never worn such brief shorts to the garden before. Today, she wore it with the sole purpose of catching his attention. And here he was, lost in thought and probably admiration for the renovated garden, seemingly unaware of her presence, let alone her long bare legs. Perversely, Meghna felt disappointed and angry. It irritated her that he was so oblivious to her while she couldn't seem to look away from his long, muscular legs exposed by the figure-hugging black shorts that he wore.

Doesn't the man have any sense of decency? All female eyes were riveted on the newcomer. Meghna gritted her teeth while she failed to notice the admiring male glances at her own legs.

Rahul walked rather stiffly as his leg brushed against Meghna's with every step they took. He kept quiet, doing his best to concentrate on controlling his hands. His body had jumped in response the moment he set eyes on Meghna that morning. Her long, slim legs appeared far too sexy. Temper flared for a moment as he thought of her contradictory words and action. She had ordered his hands off. But her clothes were too provocative, an open invitation. A smile broke out on his face as he guessed that like a typical woman, she had changed her mind and expected him to behave accordingly.

Rahul turned to his left to look at the dark brown head so close to his shoulder, her hair brushing his bare arm, slender shoulders slumped in dejection. He let go of her hand to hook an arm around her shoulders and pull her close to his body. There was no protest from her as she cuddled closer with a sigh of pure delight.

"Wonderful," whispered Rahul, close to her ear.

Meghna raised her eyes eagerly to look at his face, glad that the ice was broken. She also mentally got ready to do battle with him if he drew too close while she was inwardly thrilled with his compliment.

Rahul quickly looked away from her, pretending to admire his surroundings. "I can't believe this is the same place we used to avoid because of the mess. This garden's truly beautiful now."

He caught the look of disappointment spreading on Meghna's face as she replied in a voice totally devoid of enthusiasm, "Yeah, I know."

They walked for a while, both lost in thought. Rahul fell behind as he slowed down to appreciate the garden better. Meghna walked ahead a bit before turning around with a frown, "What's with you today, Rahul? Why are you so slow?"

"You go on ahead; I'm just admiring the view from here," he replied, a grin spreading on his face as he eyed her long legs with a look of abject pleasure on his face.

Colour flared in Meghna's cheeks. She looked around quickly to check if anyone else had heard his comment. The people around were going about their business, unaware of the undercurrents between the two of them.

She turned away from him without a reply and walked faster to put more distance between them.

"Meghna," Rahul called out. She refused to stop. "Meghna," his voice grew louder as he stepped closer, his strides not lazy any longer. He reached out to touch her shoulder. "What's eating you, honey?" His voice was too close for comfort, his soft breath stirring the tendrils of hair at her nape.

"Why? Nothing," came the innocent reply. They completed three rounds at a fast pace before descending the hill by mutual consent. They walked back to the club house in a companionable silence.

Meghna went to the changing room to pull off her shorts and t-shirt before taking a shower, all set to jump into the swimming pool. She wore a one-piece swimsuit, patterned in shades of mauve and blue with a low-cut back. The colour flattered her complexion and gave her the confidence she so badly needed just then. What she was not aware of was the way the figure-hugging suit displayed her perfectly shaped body to advantage, her legs appearing longer than ever.

Rahul—who came out of the shower at the same time that Meghna stepped out of the ladies'—couldn't help staring, just managing to stop his jaw from dropping. Was this the same chubby teenager he had left behind when he went to England?

Meghna was taller than the average woman with a slender figure, the curves in all the right places. Rahul looked at the way the bright coloured swimsuit hugged her figure lovingly like a second skin.

Meghna caught his gaze on her and moved closer to him, her eyes studying him boldly from under her lashes. He wore a brief pair of black swimming trunks, barely decent. There were more than a dozen people at the pool despite the earliness of the hour. She was glad of the distraction as a neighbour called out to her from the pool.

She had been about to make a fool of herself, being caught staring too hard at the male hunk beside her. She wondered whether he was aware of the furore he was creating among the women in the pool, and within her. She found themselves to be the cynosure of all eyes as suddenly every woman wanted to acknowledge her presence, no doubt trying to wangle an introduction to Rahul in the process.

Meghna was thoroughly exasperated and annoyed as she introduced Rahul to many of them, before she suddenly decided to call it quits and took a running dive into the deep end of the pool.

She swam furiously without a pause for about fifteen minutes, trying hard to work out the fury she felt towards Rahul. *Why does he have to preen around like a peacock lapping up the admiration of the girls like a sex-starved maniac?* thought Meghna. *So, what if they came on to him in droves? Does he have to enjoy their company so much?* Meghna was green with envy. She shuddered as she recalled the manner in which each one was vying with the others to be near him, trying to touch him wherever their hands could reach. She shook her head in a temper and swam harder.

"Ease off, honey. The swimming pool won't disappear if you slow down, I'm sure," came the taunting voice of her tormentor close to her ear.

"Get lost." Meghna spat at him.

"Meghna," Rahul placed a hand on her arm, trying to pacify her. She kicked at his chest as she swam away from him.

"Ouch," growled Rahul, his voice soft enough to be heard only by her. He was holding his chest at the point where her toes had touched him.

Meghna fell for his trick yet again as she moved swiftly over to him to inspect the harm she had done. She pushed his hand away to see for herself. Rahul pulled her close and crushed her body close to his own, pressing her head into the crook of his shoulder.

"Let me go, Rahul. This'll definitely not please your newfound girlfriends. And I'm sure I don't have to remind you to keep your hands to yourself." Meghna tried hard to sound angry, but her voice thickened as various new sensations surged through her body.

Her soft legs brushed against Rahul's hair roughened ones while her breasts were crushed against the muscular wall of his chest. Her mind wanted her to move away from him. But her body seemed to make its own decision as her arms went around his neck to hang on to him tightly, her lips pressed against the curve of his shoulder. Her tongue slowly darted out to lick at a bead of moisture on his neck, while she watched with enchantment at the pulse beating hard there, the rhythm matching her own heartbeat.

Rahul nuzzled her shoulder, his teeth nipping gently as his lips trailed a path of fire towards her ear. "I never knew sharks could exist in a swimming pool," he commented lazily, raising his head to watch Meghna with his ardent gaze.

Meghna looked up at him for a moment before burying her face in the crook of his shoulder, not able to meet the heat in his golden gaze for long. "You poor baby! I'm sure you felt terrified as they fingered you. The last time I saw, you seemed more than willing to be their meal." Her voice was mildly sarcastic as she recalled the way they had fought with each other to get their hands on him. She also recollected that he hadn't tried very hard to stop them. She pushed at his shoulders to break free of his arms as her temper built up once again. "You didn't seem to protest too hard when they fell all over you," she grumbled, her grey eyes stormy.

Rahul looked at her as his breath broke out in a sigh. His fingers played with her hair as he answered her. "They'd have clung all the harder if I had protested too much."

"Voice of experience, I presume," came the swift retort.

Rahul's eyes crinkled with laughter as he said, "Seems like I can't win either way, so what the hell?" and swept down to capture her lips in a soul-searing kiss that Meghna returned with equal fervour.

If anyone had suggested that Meghna was capable of a public display of affection a few days ago, she would have protested vehemently. But today she was only too happy to show the other girls that Rahul was interested in her and nobody else.

"Mmm, you taste delicious." Rahul traced his tongue over her lower lip as Meghna opened her heavy eyelids reluctantly to meet his laughing brown eyes. She turned away quickly, feeling shy, only to meet the interested gazes of the many onlookers standing outside the pool. Colour ran hot on her cheeks as she went underwater to hide herself. She swam below water for a while before getting out at the other end of the pool. She squeezed the excess water out of her long hair before moving towards the changing rooms. She didn't wait to find out whether Rahul had finished his swim.

They met near the lift and went up to the sixteenth floor in silence. They seemed to be in a private vacuum of their own as the conversation bounced off them, oblivious to no one but each other.

Twin tornadoes hurled themselves at them the moment Meghna opened the door to the flat. Sasha and Rehaan squealed their 'good mornings' while they were lifted and swung into the air in turn by Rahul.

Meghna went to greet Sanjay and Reema, while Rahul progressed more slowly with the kids vying for his attention. Finally, he lifted them both into his arms as he walked over to the dining table where his friend and his wife were sharing a morning cuppa.

Rahul sat with Sanjay, sipping from his mug as Meghna and Reema dealt with the children's breakfast.

"So what would you like to do today?" asked Sanjay.

Rahul hesitated for a few seconds before replying, "I'd like to go with Meghna to her class. After that we can…" he gazed at Sanjay apologetically.

"Relax, Rahul. You're on holiday. You must do what you want to."

"But so are you. And you've taken leave because of me. Sanjay, I…"

Sanjay understood only too well his friend's need to spend time with his sister. He also realised how thrilled Meghna would be to hear this. "Come on, Rahul, I'd love to spend some free time with Reema and the kids. You go ahead with your plans. It'd be great if we could all go to the *Dandiya Raas* together in the evening."

"That should be perfect. I want to tag along with Meghna wherever she goes, if she'll let me, that is. I wanna get to know her more." Rahul made his intentions clear.

Sanjay gave his closest friend a smile before saying, "Just the way to go, man. Wish you luck! I only hope she doesn't lead you a merry dance." Both men turned to look at the girl affectionately. Meghna looked up at the men's dark heads together and wondered what the two of them were cooking up between them. She raised her eyebrows in query.

Rahul gave her a sly wink before answering Sanjay from the corner of his mouth—he wouldn't be surprised if she managed to read his lips, "Don't you worry, Sanjay. I've just this minute realised that I enjoy dancing to her tunes."

Sanjay slapped his friend on his back as Rahul got up to go to his room to get ready for his outing with Meghna.

Meghna stepped out of her room ready for her classes when she noticed Rahul sitting on the sofa all dressed to go out too.

"Going somewhere?" She asked him, trying hard to hide her disappointment. *When will he return?* she wondered.

"Yes, I'm going with you, riding pillion on your bike."

Anger flared in Meghna's eyes as she bit out, "You don't trust me to ride my bike."

Rahul was in front of her in a flash. He held her face in both his hands, palms pressing hard against her hot cheeks. He waited for her to look him in the eye before saying, "You don't trust me at all, do you? Why do you always suspect my motives? Will it make you happy if I offered to drive the bike and asked you to ride behind?" he asked rhetorically.

Meghna studied his eyes for a moment before replying, "I'm sorry. Do tell me what you want to do." A charming smile replaced her tempestuous expression.

"Now, *that* would be telling," said Rahul too softly, bringing a flare of colour to her cheeks before he placed a soft kiss on her forehead. "Let's go, honey. You're getting late."

Meghna fitted the helmet on her head before gunning the engine. She waited for Rahul to sit behind her. He settled himself too close to her for comfort, his arms around her middle, his muscular chest slammed into her back, and his thighs pressed close against hers.

"Rahul," Meghna's voice rose over the sound of the engine, "I'm sure the seat has more space."

Rahul pretended to be puzzled. "So what?"

"Will you please move over a bit?" asked Meghna impatiently.

"Why? Do I make you uncomfortable?"

Meghna did not want to admit that that was exactly what he was doing. "Not really."

"Then what are you waiting for, honey? Let's go. I'm extremely comfy." He gave her his devilish grin, which seemed to be his own personal trade mark.

Meghna shot away as though her back was on fire.

Prashant was waiting for Meghna at the gates of the sports club as was his habit. A deep frown formed on his forehead when he noticed a man sitting close behind Meghna as she brought the motorbike to a stop next to him.

Rahul immediately noticed the scowl on the other man's face as he met his eyes. It was obvious, at least to Rahul, that the other man was not happy about Meghna with another man. If looks could kill, Rahul would have fallen down dead right then.

Prashant turned his gaze to look at his partner. "Good morning, Meghna."

Unaware of the animosity between he two men, Meghna returned Prashant's greeting enthusiastically, "Good morning, Prashant. This is Rahul Sinha, an old friend of the family and Rahul," she turned towards her childhood sweetheart, "This is Prashant, my partner in the dance classes." She stood back to watch the two men shake hands.

Rahul was tall and supremely confident, his handshake firm. Prashant was not so tall and rather diffident, trying hard to measure his competition while Rahul had already dismissed him as none.

"Hello," said Rahul politely, his ever-present grin absent for once while his eyes looked dangerous, even as he did his best to intimidate the other man with his superior height.

"Hello," Prashant answered with barely concealed anger and jealousy. He looked at Rahul boldly, obviously refusing to be cowed down by either his height or his expression. "Let's go, Meghna, we're getting late," said Prashant, doing his best to ignore the other man.

"Rahul," Meghna turned to look at him.

"Don't you worry your pretty head about me, honey. I'll take a round of some old haunts of mine. Should be back around eleven or so. Will that be alright?" He looked at Meghna enquiringly.

Prashant's head shot up on hearing the word 'honey'. He glared at Rahul who chose to eye him with total disregard.

Meghna smiled at Rahul, "Fine." She suddenly remembered, "Rahul, I'm not sure there's enough petrol."

"That's okay, let me handle it. Bye, honey." He called out extra loudly, succeeding in upsetting the younger man more than he already was. Rahul whistled cheerfully as he got on the bike and roared away.

"Who's he? And where the hell has he sprung from?" asked Prashant angrily once Rahul left the scene.

Meghna's glance clearly stated that it was none of Prashant's business. But she answered him patiently anyway, "Rahul is from London. He used to live in Mumbai before." She didn't elaborate further.

"What's he doing here?" asked Prashant belligerently, pushing his luck.

"He's on holiday, if it's any of your business," muttered Meghna, her temper mounting.

"But, Meghna," Prashant pleaded. "I thought you and I had an understanding. We…"

Meghna stopped walking, turned towards her partner and stood in front of him, her arms akimbo. She looked him firmly in the eye and asked, "What understanding?" her voice dangerously soft.

"Well… er…" Prashant hedged, not quite meeting her blazing eyes.

"Yeah, do tell me. I'm waiting," prodded Meghna.

"Well, everybody knows that we're a couple…"

Meghna didn't allow him to finish. "And who's everybody?" Her body was trembling in a fine fury as she fixed her tempestuous gaze on Prashant, refusing to let him off the hook.

Prashant squirmed, a flush slowly rising on his face. "Meghna, be reasonable. We, that is, you and I…"

Meghna cut him off mid-sentence once again. "Look, Prashant. Let's get this thing clear once and for all. There's no *we* as far as you and I are concerned. If, I repeat, if there's any kind of relationship between us, it's only as partners in the dance class. I've no feelings for you other than as a friend. If there's any other kind of relationship, it exists solely in your imagination. I've never encouraged you to think otherwise. I have belonged to Rahul for more than six years now." There, it was out, the verbal admission that she belonged to her tormentor.

Prashant's jaw dropped and it was obvious that he couldn't believe what he was hearing. While his eyes turned red with temper, his fists clenched tight.

Meghna could see that he was fast losing control, but she simply couldn't understand why. She had never given him the impression that she was interested in him in any other way then as a partner in the dance classes. And they were getting late for the class. She didn't want to continue discussing Rahul with him just now. The children must have already assembled in the hall. As it was, they had missed out on the warming up session they usually did before the kids arrived.

Prashant turned away from Meghna and walked to the class when it became obvious that she wasn't going to say anything more, his back stiff with hurt pride.

Meghna followed more slowly, her face disturbed, her grey eyes clouded, regretting her outburst. She consoled herself saying that it had to happen; the sooner the better, what with Prashant presuming an alliance where none existed. She shrugged her shoulders and absolved herself of all responsibility towards him. He was an adult and if he wanted to behave foolishly, it was his funeral.

Meghna walked into the class and felt infinitely more cheerful on seeing the eager faces of the kids who wished their teachers a loud, 'good morning'.

She threw herself heart and soul into the class while she realised that Prashant appeared thoroughly distracted. She first felt irritated with him and later sorry. When the kids left, she went up to him to apologise for her earlier rudeness. She called out, "Prashant."

He turned around to glare at her, his eyes spitting venom.

Meghna was shocked to see his expression and turned away, her shoulders sagging in defeat. She walked away, dejected, as she guessed that their friendship had turned sour, probably beyond redemption.

She had half an hour to wait for the next batch. Usually, she and Prashant spent the break chatting amicably over a cup of coffee. But today—Meghna shook her head to clear it. *Just forget the immature fool,* she admonished herself as she took her mobile out and dialled Rahul's cell phone, feeling glad when he lifted it on the second ring.

"Hello, Rahul."

"Hey honey! Miss me already?" came the soft, tormenting voice, right into her ear.

"Yeah," was the astonishing reply, her voice wobbly with emotion.

It disturbed Rahul. "What's it, sweetheart? Something has upset you." It was a statement, not a question.

"When'll you be back?" Meghna sounded forlorn.

"Give me five minutes, okay?"

Meghna looked at her watch to verify the time. Twenty-five minutes were left of her break. "Okay."

"See you, honey." Rahul disconnected the phone. He was standing near some shops at Dadar Circle when Meghna's call came. He had gone around to Don Bosco High School where he had studied as a kid. He had walked around aimlessly for a while, trying to recapture the feeling of nostalgia, basically killing time. He had been looking for an excuse to get back to Meghna, though her call had come as a surprise.

He turned to look at the flower shop. He had not bought flowers for anybody before. But he remembered reading somewhere that women loved receiving flowers. He thought hard, trying to recall which ones. Roses! He snapped his fingers, startling a passer-by. Yes, roses! That's what he would buy for Meghna to cheer her up. Pleased with himself on reaching this decision, he parked the bike and walked over to the shop…

…only to frown in confusion. He had felt pleased too soon, it seemed. He hadn't bargained for so many colours and variety in roses. What should he do now? He stared hard at the bouquets, scowling ferociously. The formal arrangements didn't appeal to him one bit. They appeared too artificial. He looked at the roses kept in buckets of water, segregated by their colours and sizes. He looked at the creamy roses with the baby pink centres. They looked so fresh and beautiful and guileless, reminding him of Meghna. He decided to take the risk and asked the shopkeeper to tie twenty of them into a bunch, "No plastic, please," he stated firmly. After paying for them, Rahul took the cluster of roses and got on the bike, hoping he had made the right choice.

It took him barely three minutes to reach the club. Meghna was waiting near the entrance to the hall. Was she glad to see Rahul! He got off the bike and she was amazed to see the roses in his hand. She hoped they were for her. But Rahul and flowers! She would never have associated him with such an extravagant gesture! But then, did she know him at all? "Rahul," Meghna stretched out her arms to him in greeting, her face pale and strained.

Rahul walked up to her and seeing that they had no audience, bent down to give her a brief but firm kiss on her mouth. "For you, honey," he thrust the roses at her, a trifle embarrassed.

"Oh, Rahul! This is an absolute surprise." Meghna buried her face in the soft, fragrant blooms, finding solace from the pain Prashant had inflicted on her that morning. "A lovely one!"

"Believe me, I'm amazed at myself," came the muttered response from the not-so-cool Rahul.

Meghna's face broke into a smile as she saw dark red creeping up his neck and further on to his cheeks. "Oh, Rahul! You're a romantic. I don't believe this," her voice exploded with glee.

"Romantic, my foot. I'm no sissy." But colour continued to ride high on the embarrassed Rahul's face.

"Sissy you're not, you Macho! But I do think you're a romantic at heart." Meghna leaned forward to plant a noisy kiss on his lean hard cheek before continuing, "Thank you so much for the roses, Rahul. You'll never know how much they've helped me cheer up. They look so lovely too." She touched a gentle hand to the creamy pink centre of a rose, enjoying the feel of the soft petals against her fingers.

"They reminded me of you," came the soft voice, close to her ear, his confidence regained in no time at all.

"What?" Meghna turned to look at him, startled. It was one thing teasing him, calling him a romantic and quite another, his coming up with a comment packed with passion.

"The roses," said Rahul, "they look so innocent and beautiful, just like you." His seductive voice continued to coo into her ear, making her heart explode with joy.

"Would you mind awfully, sitting through the second session?" Her eyes begged him to not mind.

"Not at all, sweetheart. I'd love to watch you dance with your two left feet," said Rahul, tongue-in-cheek.

Meghna stared at him. Yes, it was the same romantic-turned-devil, in a matter of seconds. She realised that she liked it. Very much, in fact, being romanticised a minute, teased mercilessly the next. She grinned at him before dragging him into the hall with her.

Prashant was sulking in the opposite corner.

"What gives?" asked Rahul.

"He'd somehow got the impression that he and I were a couple." Meghna's voice turned angry as she recalled their conversation of the morning.

Rahul's hackles rose, his stance possessive, "And what did you tell him?"

"To get lost. What else?"

"But why did he get that impression in the first place? I'm sure there must have been some kind of signal on your part for him to think that." Rahul had never thought of himself as a sucker for punishment. But then he hadn't realised that he was a romantic at heart, either. He couldn't seem to stop himself from asking questions about Prashant's relationship with Meghna.

"Rahul, how can you think that of me? Of course I've not encouraged him in any way. We are friends, that's all." Meghna felt tearful when she heard his sharp questions.

"Then why did he think it was more than that, Meghna?"

Meghna glared at him, her eyes shimmering with unshed tears. "How would I know, you brute? How should I know in what way the diabolical mind of a man works? I'm an ordinary, simple-minded woman," she bit out at him.

Rahul threw back his head and laughed, "Meghna, you and ordinary! You ought to be joking. Have you looked in the mirror recently?" It was obvious that he didn't mean that as a compliment. He actually sounded resentful.

Yes, Rahul was jealous of Prashant. From the moment Rahul had met the other man in the morning, he had been feeling irritated. It was obvious that Meghna spent a few hours with Prashant every day and her camaraderie with him was apparent. That it was more due to her ingenuous approach to people didn't strike Rahul. He found her extremely attractive and hence presumed that the whole male population barring her brother must find her charming too. And now it seemed that his suspicions were very much true. Prashant was attracted to her.

"Rahul," Meghna's voice was pleading. "Not you too, Rahul. I've never encouraged him, I swear. He has asked me out on a date, umpteen times. I've never gone out with him, even once."

"Then it must have struck you that he is attracted to you. Otherwise, he'll not want to date you." Rahul pointed out logically.

"Fair enough. But in what way does that conclude that I gave him reason to think that we had something going?" Meghna countered.

"Well, evidently you didn't think of breaking off your partnership," said Rahul.

Meghna was stunned. "But why, Rahul? Our profession is in no way connected to our personal lives. Why should I break off from working with Prashant when we get along so well during classes?"

"Meghna, you don't apparently know how the masculine mind works. He didn't need any other motivation."

"You're right, Rahul," said Meghna, bitterness tingeing her voice, "I definitely don't understand the male mind. What would you do if a female assistant fell for you but was excellent at her job, throw her out of her job or leave yours to join elsewhere?" she asked.

"That's different, Meghna."

"How? What's sauce for the goose is sauce for the gander, or haven't you heard?" Meghna's voice rose with her temper. She had been spoiling for a fight since the shabby treatment meted out by Prashant. Who better to argue with than dear old Rahul?

"Sweetheart," Rahul's voice softened even as hers rose, "I didn't mean it quite that way. I…"

"Then what did you mean?" Meghna's incensed voice interrupted him.

"If you'll let me finish." Rahul waited impatiently for her to say something and when she didn't, continued, "In a large office, there are too many employees. So the chances of my interacting with this imaginary female assistant are next to nil. But here, it's only you and Prashant. You surely spend a lot of time together." He could not quite control the jealousy from creeping into his voice. "So there it is, the present situation."

Meghna calmed down a bit to think with a clearer head and understood his sound reasoning. "But this is such great fun," she said wistfully.

"I know, my darling Meghna. But if the talent's there with you, I'm sure you can manage to find students anywhere you go."

"I don't believe this, Rahul. Is it really you? I was sure that you didn't have great faith in my talent. What with my two left feet?" she asked, her eyes gleaming with challenge.

Rahul grinned down at her. "But I can see that you're extremely graceful, Meghna. And your classes are packed to the hilt." Rahul was sincere in his praise.

Now, that was a compliment indeed! Meghna's eyes lit up in delight. First the roses, now this. What was happening to Rahul? She realised that it didn't really matter. Whatever it was, it was amazing. She gave him a grin before hugging him tightly. He made her feel so much better. The argument they had had over Prashant helped her see things in a better perspective.

Rahul sat back to watch in fascination as Meghna taught her class the intricate steps of the *jazzercise*. They swayed to the music, their feet tapping rhythmically. It was all he could do not to join the group. But he didn't get up from his chair as he was sure that he had annoyed Prashant more than enough for one day.

The one hour went by on wings and Meghna couldn't wait to leave. She avoided Prashant as he walked in her direction. She tucked the strands of hair that had come loose and holding on to Rahul's arm, stepped towards the entrance once the students left.

Rahul stopped her outside the doorway and asked, "Are you sure, honey? Don't you think you should make your peace with Prashant? You've a class tomorrow."

Meghna stared straight ahead; her expression mutinous. Damn Prashant! Why did he have to be such a pain? She turned around to listen to Rahul's advice and caught Prashant staring at the two of them.

She walked over to him and putting out her hand, said, "Friends?"

Prashant turned away for a few seconds. It was obvious he was having a tough time accepting Rahul in Meghna's life. He swallowed the lump which rose in his throat, took the hand she offered and replied in a gruff voice, "Friends." He looked up at Rahul and gave him yet another killing look before walking towards his scooter.

Rahul raised an eyebrow in enquiry, offering the bike keys to her. She shook her head and waited for him to start the engine, climbing behind him to hold on to him tightly, ensuring that the roses were not crushed in the process.

Sanjay and Reema opted to take a nap in the afternoon along with the children. Meghna was in her room setting her hair for the evening. Rahul was trying to get through to his father in London. A gentle smile touched his lips as he thought of his father. Shyam Sinha must be at his computer. He worked tirelessly, sometimes overdoing it. But Rahul understood and shared his father's passion for hard work.

Shyam Sinha lifted his cell phone as it rang for the sixth time. He had been too deeply engrossed in the excel sheet he had been studying and it took him a minute to come down to the present.

"Hello," he said into the phone, without checking the caller ID.

"Hi Dad. How are you?"

"Rahul, what a pleasant surprise! I'm fine, my son. How are you? How about Sanjay and his family? And how is his sister, I forget her name?"

"Meghna, Dad." Rahul tuned into his father's last question; the matter closest to his heart. "All of us are just great, Dad. So, how're you doing? Working hard as usual, I suppose. What news on Mom? Has she been bothering you?"

"Not her, Rahul. She's fine. But that girl Aisha, she has been around a couple of times, enquiring about you." His father chuckled as he recalled her visits. "She always comes in, bossing around the place as though she's already the youngest director's wife," he teased. It was obvious where Rahul's mischievous tendencies came from.

"Dad," Rahul's voice was alarmed. "I hope she has not stepped on anyone's toes." He had told his secretary, Caroline Sanders, to send Aisha away in case she turned up again. Shuddering, he recalled the day she had come into his office to meet him.

"Not to worry, Son." Shyam's voice brought him back to the present. "Caroline's quite capable of handling her. So, you tell me. How are you enjoying yourself?"

"Just fantastic, Dad." Rahul's enthusiasm came across the phone line, widening the smile on his father's face. "Sanjay's kids are too cute. They are best friends of mine now and Reema *Bhabhi's* one wonderful hostess. I do envy Sanjay, Dad." There was a wistful note in his voice.

"So, I can expect to become a Grandpa pretty soon," declared Shyam.

"Aww, Dad, don't be ridiculous. You'll need to become a father-in-law first."

"As long as you realise that, my dear son. Did I hear a wistful note in your voice just now when you were talking about Sanjay's family?"

"Well, Dad," Rahul sounded sheepish, "I feel a mite envious. Holding Sasha and Rehaan is such a wonderful experience, you know. And..." Rahul hesitated.

"And," prompted Shyam, "there's someone. So tell me about her. Is it Meghna, Sanjay's sister?" Rahul's father was not only intelligent, but meticulously logical as well. He had honed in on the change in Rahul's voice as he spoke her name and also the way he had jumped to answer Shyam's question about Sanjay's sister first.

Rahul couldn't keep the excitement out of his voice as he replied, "Yeah, Dad. I'm attracted to her immensely. In fact, I think I'm in love. But…"

"Congratulations, Rahul. I'm so glad for you. So tell me, how can I help you? Do you want me to talk to Sanjay, asking for his sister's hand? Or…"

"Don't rush me, Dad. I'm not sure I'm ready for the commitment of marriage. Please Dad. Try to understand. Being tied to someone for life terrifies me."

Shyam could understand his son's sentiments. His broken marriage to Rajni was the reason for this. He sighed. "Listen to me, Rahul. Marriages like mine aren't always the norm, where the partners are totally unsuited. You can blame neither your mother nor me completely. It's a combination of circumstances. Maybe she'd have led a happier life with another man."

Rahul wondered at his father's big heart. He knew his mother and what value she had for people. "Then how come neither of you sought to divorce? Why stick to such a farce of a marriage?" Rahul's voice was acrid as he wondered which would have been worse, a broken family or the estranged one they had become.

"Rahul," Shyam's voice was soft, "Neither of us found the need for divorce. I for one, am very satisfied with my life the way it is. I adore you, my son and my career means a lot to me. I'm extremely contented. As for your mother…"

"She's financially more than secure," interrupted Rahul fiercely. "And she has her friends. I get the picture, Dad."

"Good. You should understand that this is not necessarily the case in every home. Ours was not a love match, son. Our parents arranged our wedding. Whereas, you and Meghna should definitely have a better understanding of each other if you're both in love."

"I get you, Dad. I'll work on it. And, Dad, thanks for the advice. Love you."

"Any time, Rahul. I love you too, my son and miss you. I hope you come home soon with a bride to warm my heart."

"And Dad, please keep Aisha away from the office. She's getting to be a nuisance."

"Not to worry, Son. Take care and bye."

"Bye, Dad." Rahul disconnected his cell phone, his thoughts on Aisha. She had come to his office the day before he left for Mumbai.

Rahul was stepping out of his cabin for a luncheon appointment with a client when Aisha threw herself against him, her arms clinging to his neck.

"Rahul," she purred, "Darling Rahul, where've you been hiding? I've missed you so," she pouted.

Rahul wrestled hard with himself, trying his level best to keep the disgust from his face. He put his hands on her forearms, striving to extract himself from her clinging hold. "Hi, Aisha, this is indeed a surprise. I wasn't expecting you."

"And what if you'd been? Do you think I'd have met you?"

Not in a hundred years, thought Rahul. He admitted that she was very shrewd. But subtle, she wasn't.

"Tell me, what brings you here?" Rahul moved out of her tenacious hold, turning towards his office, breathing deeply to get rid of the smell of her cloying perfume.

"Come on, Rahul. Do you want me to spell it out to you?" Aisha followed him into his office, closing the door firmly behind her. "You must talk to that woman who calls herself your secretary. She doesn't know who I am. Rude woman! She tried to stop me from meeting you, my darling Rahul. You must tell her that we're engaged to be married. She…"

"Excuse me, Aisha. I'm not sure that I heard you right." Rahul's voice went cold, his eyes glittering gold as he tried hard to hold on to his temper. "What is it you want me to tell my secretary?"

Her blood sang in excitement when Aisha looked at Rahul. She was thrilled just looking at him. She had never met a more attractive male specimen in the whole of her life. And she had met some of the best in the world. Looking at this male hunk made her head buzz in anticipation. When he spoke, her nerves jumped in response to his sexy baritone. She was so glad that she had his mother on her side. Rajni Aunty had promised Rahul to her. So what if he resisted some? The thrill was in the chase. It didn't strike her that her quarry might not be in the run.

"*Wohi*, that we're engaged to be married." She walked towards him, trying to put her arms around him once again.

"Just a minute, Aisha. There's obviously some mistake here. I don't remember proposing to you, or is it the leap year?" Rahul was stone-faced as he bit out the words through tightly clenched teeth.

"So what, Rahul? I understand that you prefer your mother to deal with such things. Rajni Aunty has already told me how shy you are."

Rahul rolled his eyes towards the ceiling, as if he sought guidance from the heavens.

She simply ignored him as she continued, "I'm not too fussy, Darling Rahul. I've fallen for you in a big way." Her voice suggested that he was an honoured human being. "We should get along like a house on fire."

"And definitely burn to death in the process," muttered Rahul, wondering how to deal with this woman who was blessed with a rhino's hide. Nothing seemed to deter her from her chosen path. She left his mother wanting when it came to the pursuit of an object of possession. "Listen, Aisha. Let's leave my mother out of this. It's between you and me..."

"Oh, Rahul! that's so wonderful. You aren't as shy as your mother claims. You naughty boy." Rahul didn't make an effort to hide his distaste now, not that it bothered Aisha one bit. "I agree with you one hundred percent that this is between you and me. I'm glad we're on the same page." She sighed dramatically.

Rahul didn't try very hard to follow the logic in her statements before giving up on the wasted exercise.

He looked at Aisha and raised a hand to silence her before she broke into speech once again. "Just listen to me for once, Aisha." His raised his voice by a few decibels to silence her, ignoring the way she looked at him seductively, her eyes slumberous, her stance supremely confident. Rahul cleared his throat, trying to find the right words so as to not hurt her. "I think you're under a wrong impression. I don't want to get married to anyone. I'm sorry that my mother misled you into believing otherwise..."

"But, Rahul," Aisha's red mouth pouted once again, her dark eyes accusing, "I do love you so. I'm sure you aren't thinking clearly. We'll make a fantastic couple." She clasped her hands together over her ample bosom, her gaze adoring him. "Just imagine, we'll be the envy of the whole of London. We can party..."

Rahul's imagination terrorised him, drawing a clear picture of the future she described and he shuddered violently before cutting her short with a sound of disgust. "Enough, Aisha. I think we've had too much of this nonsense. I'm late for my appointment. Suffice to say that I am not, I repeat, NOT interested in you. Get that?" Rahul slammed out of his office to speak to Caroline, not waiting to hear Aisha's reply.

"I'm extremely sorry about that Rahul," Caroline apologised. "I didn't know that you were engaged." Her eyes were troubled as she looked at her young boss, feeling rather sorry for him. She thought that Aisha would make him an awful wife. But being the excellent secretary that she was, she kept her opinion to herself.

"I'm not," bit out Rahul. He looked at his secretary's startled face and patted her arm saying, "I'm sorry Caro, didn't mean to snap at you. Just ensure that that woman leaves before I return. My office is off limits to her, okay?" He smiled at her, his good humour returning.

"Gotcha, Boss. Not to worry. I'll deal with her." There was a glint in Caroline's eyes which boded ill for Rahul's unwanted guest.

He was glad to leave this particular task in the safe hands of his assistant, who was known as The Dragon very aptly.

Rahul came back to the present when he heard Meghna swear. He walked towards the open door of her bedroom to find out what was wrong. He burst out laughing when he saw her hair set in curlers. She looked up at him and joined him as his humour was so infectious.

"Rahul, you idiot. Catch you to find something to laugh about in anything and everything. Did you speak to Shyam Uncle? How's he? What's the news from London?"

"Dad's fine, thanks. I thought I heard you swear. What happened?" His curiosity got the better of him as he walked inside, moving towards her, closing the door behind him.

"Nothing much, Rahul. Only this nail polish." She made a frustrated sound. "I'm hopeless at painting my nails. Usually, *bhabhi* helps me with it. But I don't want to disturb her today as she gets so little time with Sanjay," Meghna sighed.

"Why worry about anything when I'm here?" Rahul's eyes crinkled with amusement.

"You! What do you know about painting nails?" asked Meghna, her eyes rounded in surprise.

"Come on, Meghna. I don't think it's much different from painting walls. Only the difference is in the area to be painted and the size of the brush. Believe me; I've done some painting in my time." He winked at her before squatting on the floor in front of her, crossing his legs.

Meghna, who was sitting on her dressing stool, watched in fascination as the muscles rippled on his bare legs, his shorts stopping at mid-thigh.

"Meghna," Rahul snapped his fingers in front of her eyes before turning to look curiously at her dressing table. There was a stand containing an array of nail polish bottles in various colours. An impish grin spread over his face as he asked her, "Which colour now?"

Meghna looked down at Rahul as she wiped her nails on a piece of cotton, cleaning up the mess she had made. "Are you sure, Rahul?" She asked, looking a mite worried at the devil-may-care expression on his face.

"But of course, honey. What's the harm? You can always clean it up if it's not to your liking," he pointed out logically.

"Okay." Meghna stretched out her hands in front of him after handing over a bottle of black glitter to him.

Rahul wrinkled his nose at the colour before shaking the bottle thoroughly like a professional. Meghna watched in awe as he took hold of her hand and started painting her nails meticulously with the least amount of fuss, his dark head bent in concentration. It was a relief to have his laughing eyes concentrating on something else for a change.

Meghna let out a sigh of pure bliss and gave herself up to his ministrations.

Not for long. "What are you doing?" squeaked Meghna, jumping to her feet.

Rahul lifted his face to look at her impatiently. "You do want your toenails painted, I take it?" At Meghna's nod, his frown deepened. "So why don't you let me get on with it? Just sit down, will you?" He ordered before bending down once more to continue with his task.

"Rahul," squealed Meghna once again.

"What now?" Rahul stopped his job to look up at her with a dramatic sigh, a smile lurking in his eyes.

"Can't you do that without touching my feet? I'm awfully ticklish."

"But let me first place them comfortably," said Rahul before catching hold of her right foot again.

Meghna seized his arm to stop him, a gurgle escaping her throat. "Please, Rahul," she giggled. "I can't take this. Just tell me where you want my foot. I'll place it myself."

Rahul stared at her for a few seconds before gesturing towards his folded leg. "Here."

"On your leg?" asked Meghna. She looked at him, wondering if he was joking.

"Yeah, honey. That should be best. Come on, stop being a fuss pot. I don't have all day." He moved his hand towards her foot once more as if to complete the job himself. Meghna swiftly raised her foot to place it on his bare thigh.

It was difficult to say who was more astounded at the myriad sensations building up within the two of them. Rahul looked at Meghna, his honey gaze delving deeply into her dark grey one, forgetting to smile for once in his life.Her foot felt soft against the rough contour of his thigh and sensations shot up in fine darts all through his nerves.

As for Meghna, the sole of her foot tingled at the contact with his hair-roughened thigh. Tiny sparks that began underfoot built a slow fire in her whole being.

Rahul's hand trembled slightly as he bent over to concentrate on the task at hand. He waited for Meghna to remove her right foot and place her left one in position before continuing with his work, without uttering a single word. After he finished with this, Rahul asked Meghna in a hoarse voice, barely audible, "Do you want another coat?"

She shook her head dumbly, unable to find her voice.

Rahul got up abruptly to increase the speed of the fan and walked towards the window, moving the curtain aside to look down, his fists clenched.

After about five minutes or so, Meghna walked up to him and unable to stop herself, wrapped her arms around his waist and rested her head on his back. "Thank you, Rahul." Her voice was a murmur.

Rahul turned around in her arms to hold her tightly to his chest before whispering in her ear, "You're welcome, honey, at any time." He still appeared rather dazed as he started planting tiny kisses, starting from her earlobe, moving down the length of her jaw.

Meghna turned her head to meet his teasing lips halfway, opening her mouth to give him better access.

Rahul kissed her long and hard before raising his head to look down at her flushed face, "You drive me crazy, you know."

Meghna looked at him before tracing a black-tipped finger at the Vee of his t-shirt, opening a button, her finger moving down the front.

Rahul put his hand over hers, holding it firmly, stopping her from opening the next button.

"Rahul, let me go. I want to…"

Rahul bent down to kiss her briefly, stopping her in mid-sentence before saying, "No, Meghna. Don't." He lifted the hand he was holding and placed it at his waist. "I don't think you're fully aware of what you're doing, you innocent baby."

That lit a spark of fire in her eyes. "I'm not all that innocent," she declared.

"Oh!" The ever-mobile eyebrow went up in query. "Let me hear what you've experienced," he teased.

"Why should I tell you? Are you interviewing me for some kind of a job?"

"Maybe."

"I'm not interested in working for you."

Rahul bent down close to her ear and asked her, "Then what are you interested in?"

"Going to sleep." Saying this, Meghna left his arms to go and sit on the bed. She yawned very obviously, planning to dismiss him from her room.

"Wonderful idea. Couldn't have thought of anything better myself." Saying this, Rahul plonked himself down on the other side of her bed.

"Rahul," Meghna wanted to ask him to leave but didn't have the heart to send him away.

He pulled her into his arms before tumbling them down on the bed and said, "Please, sweetheart, let me sleep with you. I promise to behave. Will go to sleep quietly holding you. No mischief, cross my heart." Rahul's brown eyes appeared molten; the heat doing marvellous things to Meghna, making her heart beat erratically.

She went into his arms willingly without as much as a word. Rahul moved to lie down with his face buried against her breasts, his arm tight around her waist.

A startled Meghna put out a hand to pull at his hair. But her hand, having a mind of its own, caressed his unruly locks, stroking rhythmically against his scalp.

Rahul sighed happily, burrowing down further. "Keep that up and I might even propose marriage," he promised.

Meghna's hand stilled for a moment before continuing its job. "Am I supposed to feel honoured?"

He opened one eye lazily to give her an upward glance. "But of course, you should. Many girls I know would give their eye-teeth to marry the handsomest guy in London."

"Is that so? I don't know. I'm interested in this guy who's the handsomest in the world." Meghna gave him a shy look before bending down to kiss him on his forehead, her hand caressing his lean cheek.

"Is that supposed to help a man go to sleep?" Rahul growled; his voice deep-throated. Both eyes were open now, bright with amusement and something else that Meghna couldn't quite identify.

"Well, I didn't raise the subject of a marriage proposal. If you thought that that would help me go to sleep, then let me tell you that you were thoroughly mistaken." Her grey eyes challenged him to get out of that one.

Rahul grinned. "Trust my dear Meghna to have a comeback for everything." He patted her cheek. "Now go to sleep," he ordered, "before I change my mind about behaving myself."

Meghna didn't need a second bidding. She closed her eyes tightly and contrary to all her expectations, went to sleep. And so did Rahul.

9

Shyam Sinha reached home at seven that evening. It was one of those rare days when he reached home early. He got out of the Mercedes Benz and bid his driver goodnight before walking up the four steps to the double doors of his house. The door opened before he rang the bell as Ramsay had been looking out for his master.

On his way to the main staircase, Shyam smiled his thanks to the butler. The house was centrally heated. *But nothing to beat a fire in the grate,* thought Shyam.

He turned around to Ramsay and said, "Do light the fire in the library, Ramsay. And set out my regular drink," smiling at him.

"Sure sir." The old butler hesitated. "Any news from Master Rahul, sir?" he asked respectfully. "How is he?"

Shyam's smile widened. "Rahul's absolutely fine, thank you, Ramsay. He called me today morning. Looks like he has found himself a girl." Shyam couldn't contain his glee. He had been dying to share that particular piece of information with someone who would understand. Who better than dear old Ramsay who was extremely fond of his young master?

"Oh, really sir? Congratulations! Should I get a bottle of champagne out of the cellar, sir?" he asked politely, unable to stop a wide smile from stretching across his serious face.

"No, no, Ramsay, not so soon," laughed Shyam. "Nothing is fixed definitely yet. I'm only guessing at things. We'll have to wait for Rahul to confirm before we celebrate. But you know how it is. With the anxiety of a typical father, I guess I got carried away. Give it a couple of days. I'm sure he'll be out with the good news by then," said Shyam, quite confident about his son's love for Meghna.

Ramsay nodded his head vigorously before saying, "Yessir."

Shyam Sinha hurried up the stairs to the master bedroom to change out of his work clothes into track pants and t-shirt before walking down to the library in ten minutes flat.

Ramsay set up a tray containing a decanter of Scotch whiskey, a couple of bottles of soda, a bucket full of ice cubes and a tall glass. He waited patiently beside the recliner to pour out the drink for his master. A fire burned cheerfully in the grate, throwing eerie shadows on the walls. Only a couple of lamps were lit in the room, behind the recliner, just the way Shyam liked it.

Ramsay had also set up the Home Theatre, which he knew his master preferred to use instead of the fifty-two-inch television that was at one end of the thirty-foot long room. The two walls along the length of the room were covered from ceiling to floor with wooden shelves containing books, giving the room its name. One rack was allotted to CDs and DVDs, to be seen and heard on the latest equipment set on a shelf with four speakers fitted at the corners of the room.

Shyam sat on the recliner, pressing the button to release the foot-rest, and leaned back with a sigh of pleasure.

Ramsay handed him the remote to the Home Theatre as he poured a measure of whiskey into the glass before looking at his master for further instructions.

"Make it a double, Ramsay, on the rocks," said Shyam, switching the various channels by remote before he found his favourite news channel.

He was feeling relaxed after a day's hard work. Usually, he went on to his club and spent the evening there. The other members were all friends and colleagues and generally tended to talk shop, which he as a rule didn't mind as he lived and breathed his work. But he wasn't in the mood for it today. He wanted to be alone and at peace. In fact, he wanted to dream about the future; of becoming a grandfather.

A smile lit Shyam's face as he sipped from his glass, inhaling the bouquet of the fine Scotch whiskey. He hadn't heard a word of what the newsreader had been saying over the past five minutes.

His peace lasted for exactly five more minutes. It was shattered by the tornado which erupted into the library in the guise of his wife, Rajni. She burst into the room and eyed her estranged husband with something akin to hatred in her eyes.

Her honey brown gaze spat venom as it moved onto Ramsay who was standing behind his master's chair at a respectable distance, waiting on him.

"Ramsay," her voice dripped ice, contradicting the fire in her eyes, "Are we paying you such exorbitant wages to be a butler or to while away your time watching the news, that too on the big screen, no less," she asked maliciously.

A ruddy colour rose up the old butler's neck as he bent his head in shame before walking out of the library without defending himself in any way, closing the door silently behind him.

Shyam watched the interplay without interrupting. It was obvious that his antagonistic wife was on a warpath and he waited patiently for her next move.

He didn't have to wait long. She pointed a shaking finger at him, saying, "You! You wily old man! What have you planned for my son? Where's he?" She moved forward into the room, her voice rising with each word.

It was obvious to Shyam that she had imbibed a drink too many and his lip curled in disgust as he watched her unsteady progress towards him. He curbed his natural instinct to get to his feet to offer his chair to her. But then, he was convinced that his wife was no lady; more of a shrew, to be precise.

"Why the sudden concern for Rahul? I've never seen you bothered about him from the day he was born," pointed out Shyam mildly, waiting for her to get to the point.

"Shyam, don't try my patience," Rajni ordered.

Shyam's eyebrow went up in an expression of surprise as if to wonder from when she had acquired that particular virtue. His supercilious facial cast only managed to fan her temper some more.

"Where have you hidden him?" she demanded to know.

Shyam shrugged his shoulders nonchalantly. "Do you think Rahul is a sack of potatoes for me to hide him where I pleased?"

Rajni didn't appreciate her husband's humour. "Don't be silly. Where's he?"

"Didn't Rahul tell you where he is? Why don't you call him and find out?" countered Shyam calmly.

Rajni appeared blank. Her son hadn't been home for three days and she hadn't missed him. She wasn't even aware whether he was in town or not, let alone that he was outside the country. "When have either of you told me anything?" she asked bitterly.

Shyam refused to respond to what he considered to be a foolish question and waited for her to continue.

"Did I hear right when I was told that he has found himself a girl?" asked Rajni, her voice a shriek, her stance belligerent.

Shyam wasn't exceptionally surprised on hearing the question. He always knew that she had her spies around the house and obviously one of them overheard the conversation he had had with Ramsay a while ago and loyally passed on the message to the mistress of the house. Rajni appeared too disturbed as she had obviously left some party in a hurry.

"So what if he has?" asked Shyam.

Sparks flew from Rajni's eyes as she glared at her husband, who sat there calmly, drinking from his glass. She controlled the mad rage that made her want to fling the contents of it on his face and hurl his glass into the fire burning away in the grate. She knew her husband of thirty-two years better than that. Words were more than what he tolerated from her, as she had found out to her humiliation. There were many temper tantrums she had controlled for fear of his retaliation. He never needed to resort to physical violence. That simply wasn't his style. He had sole control over all the bank accounts. And Rajni knew better than to argue with that.

"Shyam." Rajni's voice dripped honey in a sudden about face. She walked towards her husband very gracefully, swinging her still slim hips very delicately. She reached him and sat down on the carpet near his outstretched feet. She ran a caressing hand over his leg and Shyam just stopped himself from recoiling as if touched by a snake. He always avoided showing any emotion as far as his wife was concerned. He made an extra effort to control the revulsion pushing the bile into his throat.

"Shyam. Listen to me. You know what a darling Aisha is," she purred. "Her parents are so rich and they've an important standing in society. She'll make such an ideal wife." She looked at Shyam expectantly, sure that she could convince him.

"Well, are you suggesting that we get divorced then?" asked Shyam, his expression extremely solemn. Only Rahul would have recognised the tiny mischievous glint at the back of his father's eyes that belied the seriousness of the question.

Rajni paled visibly. "Shyam, what are you saying? Why should we get divorced?" Her voice had become hoarse, her high-flying life seeming to fade away in front of her eyes.

"Well, my dear," Shyam's voice was mildly sarcastic. "I don't know of any law that allows bigamy." He pretended to appear bemused. "Not that I want to particularly marry Aisha," he concluded, tongue-in-cheek.

Rajni looked at Shyam as if he had taken leave of his senses. But then, she could never relate to his teasing nature. "Don't be stupid, Shyam. I'm talking about Rahul and Aisha. What a wonderful couple they'd make. I can't wait to…"

"Just hold on a minute," Shyam cut her off mid-sentence. He felt sorry for her. She seemed obsessed with the idea of this match. "You heard Rahul's opinion the other day. He's not interested in Aisha. There's no point to this conversation." Shyam got up from his chair to get himself another drink, expecting Rajni to take the hint and leave. He should have known better.

"What's this I hear about *some girl* Rahul is interested in?" Rajni changed track; her expression distasteful.

Shyam looked at his wife, debating whether to tell her or not. He quickly came to a decision and sat down on the recliner. He decided to reason with her. "Look here, Rajni. Rahul's in love, I think. With his childhood sweetheart."

"Meghna," screamed Rajni. "Are you talking about that bitch Sushma's daughter? That ruthless female who stole my Rahul from me? Oh my God! My poor son! I'm sure the daughter is as bad as the mother was, if not worse. Pretending to offer love and poisoning a son against his own mother…"

"Just shut up!" Shyam's quiet admonishment stopped the tirade gushing out of Rajni's lips. "And get out of this room." He regretted his decision to talk some logic to the most unreasonable creature he had had the misfortune to meet—the one that was his wife.

Rajni stood up in a hurry, her scheming mind buzzing furiously as she walked to the door.

"And by the way, you must apologise to poor Ramsay. He doesn't deserve to be at the receiving end of your lashing tongue." Shyam's voice stopped her in her tracks. "You know better than to force my hand at choosing between the two of you," he said in reply to her unspoken query.

Shyam turned towards the newsreader who was reading out the headlines again and proceeded to push his wife out of his mind.

A seething Rajni went to her bedroom that was on the opposite wing to the master bedroom and made a call to Aisha. She told her about Rahul's visit to India and explained her next plan of action, which suited the younger girl just fine.

avratri is a much-celebrated colourful festival of India. Following the Hindu calendar, it generally falls between the latter half of the month of September and the former half of October. *Navratri* literally means nine nights.

As per Hindu mythology, Mahishasura was a demon king who ruled over the earth. He was extremely cruel and people suffered miserably under his power. He aspired to rule the Heavens and the Hades as well. Goddess Durga meditated for nine days and nights standing on one foot over the tip of a needle and conquered him on the tenth day. The nine days and nights of meditation constitute *Navratri* and the tenth day is called *Vijayadasami* or *Dasshera* meaning the victorious tenth day.

The nine days are considered very auspicious and celebrated in various fashions in the different states of India, one common thing being the worship of Goddess Durga. In states like Maharashtra and Gujarat, people get together to dance into the wee hours of all the nine nights. They get together in groups and using a pair of sticks called *dandiyas*, form circles and dance to loud music, both religious and filmy.

On this particular night in late September, Sanjay had bought tickets for all of them to attend the *Dandiya Raas* at the Parsi Club in Dadar, along with a buffet dinner. Sanjay and Rahul were ready way before the women and children.

Both the men were attired in *churidhar kurtas* made of off-white tussar silk. They wore bright coloured, embroidered waistcoats, royal blue for Rahul and a dark red for Sanjay with matching embroidered Kashmiri caps embellished with sequins decorating their dark locks and Kolhapuri slippers on their feet. Rahul sported a small, thick, gold earring on his left earlobe.

They were enjoying a glass of scotch and soda when Rehaan burst out of his bedroom. He wore jeans and a t-shirt. His face was puffed-up as if he had been crying as he ran over to Sanjay to be lifted up into his arms.

"Daddy," Rehaan buried his face in his father's neck, putting his arms around him to hold him in a tight grip.

Sanjay hugged his son close to his chest, kissing him on the top of his head. "Yeah, sonny, what's it? Have you been crying?" he asked gently.

Rehaan lifted his head to look at his father mutinously even as his lips quivered as he tried to be the perfect gentleman and not howl his heart out.

Sanjay chucked him under his chin and asked again, "Hey, buddy! What's it? Why aren't you wearing your new clothes?"

Rehaan didn't wait for his father to complete the question. His face crumpled as large tears exploded from his chocolate-coloured eyes. "I don' wanna wear it. I don' like!" He declared fervently.

Sanjay patted his son's back a couple of times before mopping his little face with a tissue. "There, darling. Don't wear the dress if you don't like it. Please don't cry, sweetheart."

Rehaan's tears stopped as if a tap had been turned off the moment his father told him that he need not wear the new dress. The child had been fascinated by the new traditional folk costume his mother bought for him. But when he wore the short shirt called *kedia* with long, tight sleeves; pleated frills at the waist; highly embroidered border and the tight trousers, he found them completely alien and wanted his mother to take them off him immediately.

The little devil Sasha had taunted him ad nauseum as he got out of the funny clothes and into the comfortable jeans and t-shirt. Hence the tears. Rehaan narrated this catastrophe in his baby language while his father listened patiently, nodding and shaking his head at appropriate intervals.

Rahul watched their interchange with great enchantment. He couldn't help smiling as he heard Sasha's role in the story.

The little girl walked out as if on cue, just as Rehaan came to the end of his pathetic story. He let out a murderous yell as he caught sight of his sister and jumped out of his father's arms. He went to her in a flash and pulled at the red satin ribbon which was intricately woven into her dark curling hair.

Sasha shrieked before hitting her little brother hard on the hand which was pulling at her precious ribbon.

Both the children raised hell in the few seconds it took for Sanjay to separate them.

"Quiet," ordered Sanjay, without raising his voice.

Rahul was amazed at how the squabbling children calmed down immediately, at their father's command.

But the peace lasted for only a few seconds. Pandemonium broke out as both started yelling simultaneously, at the top of their voices, complaining and calling names.

Sanjay raised his eyes heavenwards before sharing an amused glance with Rahul. Then he turned towards the kids and asked very softly, "Shall we go to the *Dandiya Raas* or cancel the programme?" The shock worked wonders. "Now listen to me, you little guys. Rehaan will go in jeans and t-shirt as he's more comfortable in them." Rahul wondered how Sanjay managed to keep the laughter out of his voice as Sasha made a monkey face on hearing this. "Sasha, you have to stop bothering Rehaan."

"But Daddy, his new dress is so cute. He…"

Rehaan shook his fist at her.

Sanjay spoke once again. "Listen, Sasha Darling. Rehaan doesn't like it. And we'll not force him to wear it. Now let me look at your dress." He distracted her attention away from his son. "You look very sweet."

Little Sasha turned around to look at Rahul for approval. She wore a traditional *ghaghra choli* in a bright shade of red with golden sequins shimmering all over every time she turned. She did a pirouette that billowed the ankle length skirt for Rahul's benefit. She had matching red ribbon in her hair which was still intact—no thanks to Rehaan—and red shoes on her tiny feet.

"You look so cute," said Rahul as he bent down to meet her at eye level. He leaned forward to receive a wet kiss from her for his efforts.

Then he turned around to look at the now silent Rehaan. They studied each other for a while before Rahul threw open his arms to the little fellow. The child ran into them as Rahul lifted him high above his head, tickling him.

Rehaan giggled, clinging to Rahul's neck. He touched the bright blue cap on the man's head with great interest. Rahul asked him, "Do you want to wear it?"

Rehaan shook his head firmly before saying, "No" as he wiggled out of Rahul's arms. He ran into his room and brought out a similar blue cap, much smaller in size, and placed it on his own head, grinning at the older man.

Rahul smiled back at the little guy, gently adjusting the cap to the back of his head before solemnly shaking hands with him.

Both Meghna and Reema walked out of their rooms from the opposite ends within a moment of each other. The men looked on, turning their heads from side to side, their mouths hanging open.

It was obvious that the women had gone to a lot of effort to achieve a fabulous effect. They reached the middle of the drawing room and twirled around for the men's benefit.

Reema wore a designer *ghaghra choli* in a combination of burnt orange and hot pink with gold *jardousi* work. She wore chunky gold jewellery to match, long dangling earrings, necklace and gold bangles interspersed by coloured metal ones of orange and fuschia. Orange *mojiris* with gold embroidery enclosed her feet and she looked stunning. Sanjay walked over to her and kissed her lightly, his eyes gleaming with love.

But Meghna stole the show in her black chiffon *anarkali* suit over a lining of silver glitter. The top flowed down to a couple of inches above her ankles while the *churidhar* cuff of black peeped above black and silver *mojiris*. The black set off her golden colour while she appeared taller than ever in the outfit. Her silky brown hair was a tumbling mass of curls arranged beautifully around her radiant face. Large, silver hoop earrings hung from her delicate shell-like ears. A matching necklace encircled her slender throat, while silver bangles jingled on her arms. The back of the top was cut deep, almost to her waist while it was held together with silver strings knotted down her spine from shoulder level to the middle of her back. She wore a *dupatta* of silver net on one shoulder.

Her make up was light. A *tikli* of black and silver shone in the middle her forehead. Pale silver glitter shadowed her eyelids with dark brown outlining her eyes. A pale blush highlighted her cheekbones and a natural shade of lipgloss completed the make up.

Rahul stared at her before blinking his eyes a couple of times to clear his vision. No, she wasn't a figment of his imagination. His face broke into a smile as he walked closer. She stood still, blushing to the roots of her hair, waiting for his compliment.

Rahul lifted her hands to his lips before commenting, "Now I can see why you chose the black nail-polish. It's perfect."

Meghna raised astounded eyes to his face and stared enchanted at the gold ring in his left ear. He looked wild and untamed.

Rahul felt himself drawn into the grey pools that were her eyes as she stared at him beseechingly. They invited him to tell her how lovely she looked. But all he felt was panic at the thought of commitment. The Rahul of the afternoon seemed to have disappeared with the setting sun. This man wanted to simply turn tail and run. He forced himself to turn away from the ravishing woman who was slowly but surely taking over his heart. Instead, he looked at Reema and said, "*Bhabhi*, you look amazing."

Rahul couldn't help but notice the hurt in Meghna's eyes and felt like a rat. Feeling forced to acknowledge her magnificent looks, he spoke without thinking, "Meghna, contrary to popular belief, fine feathers do a peacock make. You look wonderful in that get up."

He realised his mistake the moment lightning struck at him from laser sharp grey eyes. He had done it now. Opened his big mouth—no, his goddamned big gaping hole of a mouth and put not one, but both of his size eleven directly into it. Fool that he was! If anyone was handing out awards for idiots, he would definitely find himself at the top of the line.

Rahul! He mentally shook himself. *Grow up man! You aren't a teenager anymore,* he chided himself. All of thirty and a few months to spare. What had come over him? That afternoon, he had as good as told Meghna that he wanted to marry her. No wonder she looked so hurt at his inane comments.

Meghna looked at the silent Rahul beside her from the corner of her eyes. But his poker face told her nothing about the turbulent state of his mind. She turned away from him abruptly to walk towards her nephew and niece. "Sasha sweetie pie, come to Meghna Aunty. Let me see your new dress."

The young lady had been admiring her mother's outfit. Now she turned around and ran to her aunt.

"Wow, baby. You look gorgeous." Meghna bent down to press her hot cheek against Sasha's cool one, trying hard to bring her hurt expression under control.

Creep! That's what he was. She didn't give a damn what he thought of her looks. She didn't care. She had checked herself out in the full-length mirror before she stepped out of her room. She knew she looked fantastic and she didn't need him to tell her that. *But I went to so much effort exclusively for him.* A small voice in her head reminded her. Meghna shook her head hard to clear it.

"Rehaan, sweetheart, come here," she called out loudly to drown the voice in her head. "That's a lovely cap you're wearing. You look so handsome." She kissed her nephew's cheek as he grinned his pleasure at her generous compliment. She tactfully didn't speak about the new dress which was nowhere in sight.

She moved forward to tuck her hand into Reema's before turning around and asking of no one in particular, "Shall we leave?"

Reema got into the front of the Fortuner next to her husband. Meghna insisted that both the children sit in the back along with her and Rahul. The latter tried his level best to catch her eye, to no avail. She refused to even look in his direction. Reema was aware of the undercurrents as she looked at her sister-in-law's pinched face. She said nothing as her blissfully unaware husband reversed out of the parking lot, whistling a popular tune.

They reached the club soon but it was a while before Sanjay could find a parking space. He locked the vehicle and all of them walked to the entrance, the kids chattering excitedly.

Sanjay was speaking to Rahul and was getting terse monosyllables in response to his efforts. Reema and Meghna stuck together as the older woman put an arm around the younger one's shoulders, doing her best to cheer up the younger woman.

"*Bhabhi*, do you really think Rahul is interested in me?" Meghna's voice was choked with emotion as she sought reassurance.

Reema looked at her sister-in-law with compassion in her dark gaze. "I'm sure of it, Meghna. He looks as if he's struggling with himself. Why don't we wait and watch?" They spoke in an undertone to not let the others hear them.

It was all easy for Reema to say, but Meghna was on pins. She had been sure Rahul was attracted to her, especially after the wonderful afternoon they spent together. But he had been so unimpressed with her looks after she had gone to so much effort. Why the hell was he playing fast and loose? She didn't respond to Reema, refusing to be pacified. Her temper was too high.

And who was the first person they met on entering the grounds? None other than Prashant. The expressions on the faces of the four adults were varied. So were their reactions.

"Prashant! This is a surprise! How're you?" asked Sanjay, his usual jolly self, greeting his sister's colleague of long standing with enthusiasm.

"Hello." This was Reema's low voice, trying hard to hide her chagrin. *Meghna didn't need this puppy dog hanging around her today of all days,* she thought.

Rahul nodded his head curtly, a scowl drawing his thick eyebrows together, his golden gaze spitting fire at his adversary. What was this oaf doing here? He needed him just now like he needed a hole in his head.

Meghna caught the expression on Rahul's face and turned towards Prashant with a wide smile. "Prashant," she drawled, "this is a lovely surprise. You never told me that you were coming here this evening." She took his hands in both of hers and looked up into his startled eyes, and gave him a broad wink.

His eyes bulged out from their sockets as he stared in shocked surprise at the transformation in her demeanour. "Meghna," he gasped in a choked voice, "you look wonderful."

This was too much for Rahul. He stepped forward to put a proprietary arm around Meghna's waist. He bent down and whispered in her ear, "You're making an exhibition of yourself, Meghna. We're blocking the entrance. Let's go inside." He ignored the flames leaping into her eyes as he moved forward, dragging her along with him, without bothering to find out if the others were following.

Reema was glad to see Rahul taking the situation into his hands. She had been worried at the way Meghna had greeted the puppy dog. With that fear out of the way, she looked forward to the evening with more cheer. She gave Rahul the thumbs up when he finally turned to look for them.

Rahul didn't need a second bidding. He walked swiftly, dragging the visibly reluctant Meghna along with him. They walked through the crowd and reached an empty table for two. They plonked down heavily as if they had just completed the marathon.

"Rahul Sinha," Meghna spoke in an angry undertone, "I hate you. How dare you?" Her slender frame shook with a fine temper, her curls bouncing around her head, her stormy grey eyes accusing. "How dare you treat me like a child? Didn't you see that I was talking to Prashant?"

Rahul picked up a couple of glasses of cold drinks from a passing waiter. He turned to look at her, his own eyes blazing golden, ready to let rip. But the moment he laid his eyes on her beautiful but stupendously angry face, he felt his own temper evaporating as dew in the face of sunbeams. His eyes cooled down to the shade of molten honey and they crinkled into a smile as he looked at the girl of his dreams with an adoring expression. "Meghna, listen to me…"

"Aw, shuddup, Rahul! You are a big fat bore," she declared violently.

"Big, I agree. Bore, I'll accept. But fat? Come on, Meghna. By no stretch of imagination can you call me fat," said Rahul in a pleading voice, an appealing expression on his face, his hand placed beseechingly on her arm, a smile lurking in the depth of his eyes.

His words drew her attention to his whipcord frame clothed in the traditional Indian wear. He was too attractive for his own good, she thought. She stared at him, the fire in her eyes banked for the moment, wondering what to make of him. She was getting rather tired of this cat and mouse game he was playing. He was obvious angry that she had spoken gushingly to Prashant. Meghna turned red at the thought. What a foolish thing to do! Just that morning, she had warned Prashant off. But a few minutes ago, she had greeted him like a long-lost lover. How stupid could she get? Didn't she have more sense than to awaken a sleeping tiger?

But then, she wanted to blame it all on Rahul. He had driven her up the wall with his crazy behaviour. What was wrong with the man? She had made such tremendous effort to get all decked up for his sake. She had never taken so much trouble over her appearance, ever before. And look at him; he behaved like he was blind.

A sudden thought struck her. Was he otherwise inclined, by any chance? Laughter bubbled in her throat at this notion. Of course not! He was as normal as they came; quite a red-blooded male, in fact. Look at the way he reacted when she spoke to Prashant. He had been enraged. And there was the way he had kissed her at the swimming pool that very morning. Her whole body heated up while her lips tingled as she recalled their torrid kiss.

Just now, she gave Rahul a surreptitious look from under her long lashes to find him studying her intensely. She lowered her lashes in a hurry. If it had made him jealous, then something worthwhile had come out of her meeting with Prashant. She felt a trifle ashamed at the careless fashion in which she had treated the younger man, deciding to apologise to Prashant at the earliest possible opportunity.

Rahul watched the expressions chasing one after the other across Meghna's revealing face. He couldn't move his gaze away from her animated face. He was a goner all right and he might as well accept it. His heart increased pace, even as his breathing turned shallow. *Not today. Let me enjoy my freedom for another twenty-four hours.*

Tomorrow, he decided, tomorrow he would take her out on a date and propose marriage after declaring his love—in private. Not here where there were at least a couple of thousand people thronging the grounds waiting for the band to start playing music.

Rahul felt relieved on reaching that particular decision. He took Meghna's hand in his and said, "Meghna honey! I'm sorry for being such a heel. Forgive me?"

His little-boy expression made Meghna smile despite herself.

"Thanks, sweetheart." He blew her a kiss. "Now let's start from the beginning. You look fabulous. Quite sexy, actually. I'm having a terrible time keeping my hands to myself." Speaking in a hoarse whisper, Rahul watched colour flaring on Meghna's cheeks. "Will you please be my dance partner for the evening?"

Meghna gave him a small nod, unable to find her voice. She felt as though the carpet had been pulled out from under her feet. What was with him? She wondered. He blew cold and then he blew hot. She shrugged her shoulders philosophically, deciding to enjoy the evening to the full.

Neither of them noticed that Prashant fumed in silence as he drank from his glass, his black eyes following Meghna and Rahul as they walked towards a table. For a minute, when Meghna greeted him at the entrance, he had thought that his life was back to normal. It had been obvious that she was glad to see him. And then Rahul had come and spoilt everything. What power did he have over Meghna?

From his viewpoint, Prashant felt that Meghna would have been content to settle down with him, but for the advent of that villain from London. Why couldn't he have remained where he was? What was the need for him to come here and spoil Prashant's relationship with Meghna? Since many weeks, Prashant had been planning to meet Meghna socially at this very *Dandiya Raas*. But his relationship with Meghna—what there had been of it—had fallen apart because of the unexpected arrival of Rahul Sinha. Prashant gritted his teeth as a wave of anger overcame him. How could he get Meghna back? Was it even possible? He refused to think otherwise.

11

The scene was a classic fusion of the Orient and the Occident. The clothes—Rahul couldn't remember ever seeing such variety and colour at one single venue.

The men were dressed in smart casuals, semi-formals as well as Indian formals. Colourful waistcoats vied with short embroidered *kedias*. Many sported colourful caps or turbans.

As for the women's attire, the choice was mind blowing. Jeans with embroidered hems teamed with short colourful tops, *ghaghra choli, salwar kameez*, sari—you name it and someone was wearing it.

They all blended into a kaleidoscope of art and colour and the overall effect was a pleasing eyeful.

Then there was the music. Indian folk music, music adapted from Bollywood and of course disco music. The crowd went crazy as the band started playing. They separated into groups and formed circles, each holding a pair of sticks or *dandiyas*.

They began dancing, holding a wooden *dandiya* in each hand, clicking the sticks against each other or those held by their partners. The clacking of the *dandiyas* formed a rhythm and the dancers moved ecstatically in time to the music.

Sanjay and Reema, along with the kids, joined a circle in the centre of the ground. This had many children of similar age as Sasha and Rehaan.

Rahul and Meghna got together with a group of strangers and swirled to the music, clacking their *dandiyas* away, swinging to the rhythm. They both were excellent dancers, as they naturally enjoyed dancing. They were too absorbed in each other to be aware of the rest of the crowd. They were completely unaware of Prashant watching them avidly, raw hunger in his eyes as he devoured Meghna's graceful movements. His expression changed to one of hatred every time his eyes fell on Rahul.

The next hour flew away on wings as Meghna twisted and turned, moving forwards and backwards in the circle, her eyes on Rahul's animated face. His face was alight with the joy he felt swaying his body to the high-pitched folk music. Then it suddenly changed to a disco number and the crowd danced at a frantic pace. The two of them gave themselves up to the pace set by the band, now fast, now slow.

A short break was announced when the crowd rushed towards the stalls set up for food and drinks. Rahul and Meghna stood back to let the others move ahead. Rahul put his hand around Meghna's waist and gently wiped her perspiring face with a snow-white handkerchief which he removed from his *kurta* pocket.

Meghna gave a sigh of contentment as he smiled at her. "So tell me; how do you feel now?" he asked, an eyebrow raised in query.

"Simply awesome," she responded in a whisper, as he leaned down, thrusting his ear close to her mouth to catch the soft words. Meghna placed her left hand on the nape of his neck to hold him in place and further cooed in his ear, "That gold earring of yours looks sexy," smiling into his startled gaze.

He gave her a broad grin saying, "Well thanks, kind lady, you've made my day." He pressed his lips to her hot cheek for just a second before raising his head to look at her face with dancing golden-brown eyes.

Meghna felt her heart overflow with the love she felt for him. She did understand to some extent the struggle he had had to undergo to come to terms with his attraction for her. She knew about his insecure childhood and could well understand his fear of commitment. But he had reached a decision, it seemed. He appeared more peaceful than earlier. Her eyes shone with excitement as the band struck again.

They continued to dance to the music, taking short breaks to quench their thirst and nibble on some snacks. Just before midnight, Sanjay and Reema were ready to leave as the children were sleepy.

Rahul and Meghna opted to stay back. They were charged with excess energy and danced ceaselessly, oblivious to the thinning crowd around them. They had dinner at two am, totally absorbed in one another, not quite aware of what they ate.

Finally, they went home by cab half an hour later. Rahul took the key Meghna held out to him and opened the door to the flat. He closed the door quietly and not bothering to switch on the light, pulled Meghna into his arms. He led her to the sofa and settled on it, holding her in his lap.

He pressed his lips to the curve of her neck in a hot kiss. "I so wanted to kiss you all evening," he murmured. His hands moved restlessly over the bare skin of her back, the knot at her nape disturbing his caresses, an invitation to be pulled open.

Meghna held on to his neck with both arms tightly wrapped around him, her face buried in his chest, her left ear pressed against his wildly beating heart.

"Meghna honey, you're driving me nuts," he continued the whispered, one-sided conversation, his lips brushing against the shell-shaped whorl of her ear. He raised his head to look down at her dark head. He touched his forefinger to her earring, swinging it back and forth with the movement of his finger. "Will you get this damned thing off your ear?" He growled suddenly.

Meghna lifted her head, startled, slumberous eyes searching his face. His eyes appeared more gold than brown in the eerie light coming through the windows. She lifted her hand to pull off the offending piece of jewellery. The next second Rahul swooped down to nip at her soft earlobe with his teeth. He pressed Meghna's head swiftly into his chest to muffle her startled exclamation. He rubbed his tongue gently against the earlobe making murmuring sounds of apology, his tongue further tracing the shape of her ear as he blew gently into it.

Meghna's body shuddered with pleasure. She had been startled at first by the sharp nip she felt on her ear. But now she felt herself drowning in the sensations Rahul created with the attention he was paying to that particular part of her anatomy.

"Witch," came the low-pitch of his caressing voice. Rahul dragged his lips down her cheek, moving towards the other ear. Meghna accommodated him by promptly removing the other earring.

She turned this way and that trying to catch his wayward mouth that seemed to settle on every feature other than her lips.

His left hand moved from her back, stroking her hip, and down her leg before finally settling on her foot. He removed her shoe and slowly rubbed her extremely sensitive instep with the pad of his thumb.

She was at the total mercy of the sensations he aroused in her. After trying hard to get him to kiss her, Meghna raised her head to kiss his right ear. Her tongue ran in and out of his ear and she felt thrilled when she heard him groan with desire. She gently sunk her pearly white teeth into his earlobe and tugged on it.

"Meghna," came the muffled protest as Rahul felt himself losing control. "Honey, stop that."

"Why? I like it. Don't you?" she asked throatily, not quite aware of the power she wielded over him. She gazed at him, her trusting grey eyes brimming with love.

Rahul looked down at her, his body protesting at the torture it was undergoing. "Time to go to bed, Meghna."

"Yours or mine?" she asked, giving him a naughty glance.

"You shameless hussy! You go to yours and let me go to mine."

"Not yet," Meghna pouted, shaking her head.

"Please honey, it's past three. Sanjay or *bhabhi* could walk in on us any moment."

Meghna put her arms around Rahul's waist and held on tight. "No. Otherwise," she looked at him, "you come to my room. You can leave whenever you want." She gave him her permission, like royalty.

"Meghna," Rahul tweaked her nose. "Listen to me, honey. You…"

"No." This time the protest was impassioned. Idiot. Why could't he just shut up and kiss her? Couldn't he see that she so badly wanted him to? Instead of which he wanted her to go to bed, alone.

Rahul grasped that the matter was slightly outside his comprehension. He stared down at her head, a gentle smile curving his lips. He bent further down and spoke into her ear, "What is it, my love?"

Meghna lifted her face once again to look at him, her eyes pleading, "You should know."

"So, I don't. You tell me." Rahul's countenance broke into a smile when he realised that she wanted him to kiss her on her mouth, but was feeling too awkward to tell him in so many words.

"Rahul, please…" the words stuck in her throat. *How does a girl ask a guy to kiss her? Doesn't he know?* All the heroes of the romantic novels she had read seemed to know instinctively when the heroine wanted to be kissed. But, Rahul, she sighed, Rahul was *one of a kind*, will never confirm to any rule.

"Please what, Meghna?" He asked patiently, as if he had all the time in the world, when he was the one who had reminded her that it was getting late.

She frowned at him for a moment wondering how to get the message across. It never even struck her for a minute that she could have left him right then and there and gone to bed. She wanted him to kiss her and she refused to give up.

Rahul looked on with great absorption, fascinated with the way she was trying to work around her problem, her teeth worrying her lower lip, a fierce frown of concentration on her forehead.

Suddenly her face brightened as she seemed to strike upon an idea, and she raised her eyes to his, her grey gaze challenging him to get out of this one. She lifted her arms to lock them around his neck and pulled his head down towards her and pressed her lips to the corner of his, her gaze triumphant as it met his.

He stared back at her and with great difficulty controlled his body from reacting. His lips twitched as they wanted to take over and kiss her senseless. But he waited with an outward calmness which he was far from feeling, wondering how far she would go.

Meghna was puzzled at his lack of reaction. What was wrong with the man? He was the one who had got her hooked on to this kissing business, and now why was he behaving like he couldn't care less? But she wasn't going to give up, not after coming this far.

In fact, Rahul was banking on that very quality of hers.

Mehgna moved her lips over his, her pink tongue darting out to stroke against his lips, tracing their masculine shape.

Rahul was hard put to control his rising blood pressure.

Meghna moved away a couple of inches to look for his reaction. His eyes were closed while hot colour raged in his cheeks. She placed both her palms against his cheeks to hold his face and was thrilled at the heat which hit her palms. A small, self-satisfied smile stole over her face and before giving herself time to think, she raised her head and bit his sensual lower lip sharply.

"Sss…" Rahul lost his cool as he took over and kissed her mercilessly, his tongue plunging deeply into her welcoming mouth.

Meghna moaned in contentment as she finally got what she wanted.

It was after a long time and with great difficulty when Rahul prised his mouth from hers, cutting off the kiss despite Meghna's protest.

"Bed for you, young lady." He lifted her in his arms and strode towards her bedroom, kicking the door open with his foot. He stood her on the floor beside the bed and switched on the table lamp.

He looked at her in the golden glow. Her hair was a tumbled mass of curls. Her grey eyes were sparkling alive with excitement. Her rosy red lips were parted, swollen from his kisses. His arms automatically went around her, his mouth finding hers once again.

"Please, Meghna." His lips traced a path to her ear again. "Wish me goodnight."

"Sleep with me, Rahul, please," she begged.

"No, Meghna." His protest was sharp.

"But you did, this afternoon," she pointed out innocently.

"This afternoon—well, that was a long time ago. And now is now. No, Meghna." Rahul's voice was firm.

"Why?"

Rahul sighed. "Believe me, it's easier to handle Sasha's and Rehaan's 'whys'. Let me go, Meghna," he insisted.

"No, I don't want to." Meghna's face turned mutinous.

"Honey, what do you know about the male anatomy?"

Meghna looked at him silently, wondering what he was getting at. "Why the biology lesson so early in the morning?" she asked.

"After the kind of dancing we did and the way we kissed each other in the hall just now, I'll not be able to *sleep* with you, Meghna. I won't be able to stop myself from making love to you." Not seeing any light of understanding on her face, he added, "Completely."

Much to Rahul's delight and amusement, a crimson blush stole over Meghna's cheeks as she caught on. She buried her face in his broad chest and uttered a muffled "Sorry."

"Don't be. I'm just glad you trust me so much. Now, may I go?" He removed his arms from around her as he placed a chaste kiss on the top her head. "Or would you rather I stayed back and helped you untie the complicated knots on your *kameez*?"

"Yes please," came the squeaky answer, as Meghna turned around, presenting her back to him.

Rahul pressed his lips to the side of her neck, his arms going around her once more. He pulled at the knot with his teeth, his lips tracing a path of fire over the smooth skin of her back. Meghna felt too weak to protest as his hands rose to cup around her breasts. Strange sensations floated in her body as he touched her in a way she had never been touched before.

Her head fell back against his shoulder as he moved his hands restlessly against her *anarkali* top. Rahul wondered whether he would make it to his bed at all. He felt extremely reluctant to part with Meghna.

"Tell me to leave, Meghna," he whispered against her jaw line. "Please."

Meghna realised that he was fighting for control. She gently pulled his hands away from her protesting body and stepped away from him. "Goodnight, Rahul darling." She blew him a kiss, "Sweet dreams."

"Goodnight, honey," said Rahul for the nth time before moving swiftly out through her door. He put his head back inside for a moment to say, "Do lock your door, just in case." He gave her a broad wink before pulling his head out and closing her door firmly behind him.

Meghna stared in his wake for awhile, grinning broadly. She felt delirious with happiness. Rahul! Her darling Rahul! Finally, she felt she belonged to him. Her face coloured as she gently pulled off her top. She stepped out of her *churidhar*, and straight into the bathroom.

She opened the shower and let the sharp needles of water stroke her as she felt a new awareness of her own body. It felt like a stranger had taken her place. She felt wicked as she soaped herself, running caressing hands all over her person, feeling her skin tingle with raw energy.

She stepped out of the shower after shampooing her hair and rinsing it thoroughly. She wrapped a towel around herself and walked into her bedroom and looked at the bed.

She felt wide awake. No point in going to bed. It was almost 5 o'clock. She felt totally recharged. She decided to surprise Reema by preparing breakfast and lunch.

She went to her wardrobe and pulled out her brightest clothes—a pair of sunny yellow shorts and a white t-shirt patterned in yellow, green, and orange. She dressed quickly before setting her hair with a hair-dryer. She smiled at herself in the mirror as she realised that all the curls had straightened out. She pulled her hair into a high ponytail and secured it with a scrunchie. Slipping her feet into a pair of brilliant pink rubber sandals, she went into the kitchen to begin her day.

She switched on the music system and kept the sound low so as to not disturb the others. She hummed along as she set to work. The coffee filter was bubbling happily when she started roasting semolina to make *upma* for breakfast. She removed the plastic container of shelled peas that Reema usually stored in the freezer and another container of grated coconut. She removed some carrots and beans from the refrigerator. Armed with some tomatoes, potatoes, and onions, she set to work happily, chopping the vegetables. She grinned crazily at the plants Reema grew on the window sill as the golden glow of dawn shimmered through the west facing window.

Meghna stored the piping hot *upma* in a hot case before placing all the ingredients for the coconut chutney in the mixer, to grind later. Once the milk was heated, she made herself a cup of coffee and sat on the cane swing in the hall, looking through the window at the awakening world.

After the relaxed cup of coffee, she went back into the kitchen to get lunch ready. She found kidney beans soaked in water. She put that in the pressure pan to cook the children's favourite *rajma*. She kneaded some dough of self-rising flour to make hot *naans* later. She shredded spinach to make *palak paneer*, a dish of spinach and fresh cottage cheese. She was humming contentedly to herself, unaware of the passage of time.

It was gone seven when a startled Reema found her sister-in-law working hard in the kitchen, singing to herself.

"*Bhabhi*," Meghna protested. "This is supposed to be your morning in bed. Please go back and let me serve you and Sanjay coffee there."

Reema studied the younger woman's glowing face for a moment before asking, "Has he popped the question yet?"

Meghna blushed a fiery red before shaking her head, "Not yet, *Bhabhi*."

"Which means very soon," declared Reema.

Meghna nodded shyly as Reema gave her a hug.

"Congratulations, my dear. It's high time."

"Thank you, my dear *bhabhi* and now off with you. Go back to bed. Let me indulge you for a change."

"That you do anyway on all weekends, Meghna. But today's a special day for you. You shouldn't be working so hard," protested Reema.

"But *Bhabhi*, I'm too excited to sleep. I feel revitalised. What better way to shed off this energy than to work in the kitchen?"

"You mean you haven't slept at all?" asked the intrigued Reema.

Meghna gave her a mischievous grin before saying, "Nope. It was quite late when we returned. Or should I say early morning. Then I had a shower and felt too wound up to go to sleep." Meghna blushed once again as she could see from Reema's expression that her brother's wife could read pretty well between the lines.

Meghna shooed her sister-in-law back to her bedroom before arranging a tray with a jug of coffee; a bowl of sugar; mugs and spoons. She walked over to her brother's bedroom and knocked before entering.

Sanjay opened his arms wide to give her a hug after she placed the tray on a side table. "Congratulations, sweetie," he said, before kissing his sister on her forehead.

Meghna felt as if her face had permanently changed to the colour of beet. She sat on one corner of the bed and poured three mugs of coffee before passing a cup each to Sanjay and Reema. She shared a few precious moments with them before the children woke up.

The household was alive with chatter, what with the squabbling kids and Sanjay and Reema busy making tentative plans for the day. Meghna kept glancing at Rahul's bedroom door from time to time, willing it to open. *Should I go in and wake him up?* she thought. Then she shook her head to herself. *Let him sleep.* It was barely nine and he had gone to sleep only in the early hours of the morning.

But she didn't want to have breakfast without him. Meghna realised that she didn't want to do anything that would take her away from her precious Rahul. She wondered whether he felt the same way about her.

Without stopping to think, she walked into his room to find the bed empty. She could hear the shower running in the bathroom and decided to wait for him there. She made the bed, folding away the sheets and looked around for any other clutter. The room was very neat except for a few signs of occupancy. The ever-meticulous Rahul—just her opposite.

She heard the water stop running and turned away to the window. She moved back the curtain a few inches and looked down on the swimming pool, staring with unseeing eyes.

The object of her thoughts towelled himself dry while whistling a popular tune. His thoughts were filled with Meghna. He couldn't help smiling when he thought of their parting the night before. Both had been extremely loath to leave the other. He couldn't wait to meet her again. Oh, God, she felt so perfect in his arms. He stepped out of the bathroom in a rush, wrapping the towel around his waist.

Rahul felt Meghna's presence in his bedroom even before he saw her at the window. His eyes lit up with pleasure when he saw her slim, long, bare legs. He walked over and slid his arms around her before greeting her, "Good morning, honey," softly in her ear.

He smelt fresh from the shower, his hair still damp. Meghna turned around and sliding her arms around his waist, buried her face against his bare chest, wishing him a muffled, "Good morning," in return. She loved the feel of his silken body hair against her face.

Rahul felt peace seep through him as he held her soft body close to his own hard one. She felt perfect in his arms and he realised that he wanted her to become a permanent feature in his life. Gone were the days of his bachelordom. He didn't crave for them any more. He was more than ready to become a married man and raise a family of his own. This thought gave birth to a new one. He wanted to become the father of Meghna's children, and how! A couple of tiny tots with dark brown hair and stormy grey eyes danced before his vision and his arms tightened around the woman who was responsible for his day dream.

Meghna looked up at him questioningly and Rahul was shocked to see her blood shot eyes.

"What's it, honey? Have you been crying?"

Meghna frowned at him, a question in her own eyes, before shaking her head vigorously, *"Nahi toh?"*

Rahul's forehead pleated in a frown of anxiety, "Your eyes are bloodshot."

"Oh that! That's because I'm feeling sleepy."

"Then why did you get up? You should've stayed back in bed." Rahul sounded puzzled.

"But I never went to bed," smiled Meghna despite her tiredness.

"What?" barked Rahul. "Why?"

Meghna looked at his concerned face, her grey eyes dancing with mischief. "Now who's sounding like Sasha and Rehaan?" she asked. Then seeing the fire in his gaze, she added hurriedly, "My bed felt too lonely. So I decided not to sleep."

"Meghna," Rahul was exasperated. "Now you're being unreasonable, honey. You…"

"Rahul," Meghna interrupted him, her face serious. He watched the change in expression warily. "Rahul," she repeated, "will you stop reading me a lecture and give me a kiss?" she demanded. "What's the world come to, I wonder. Girls having to beg guys to ……mpft."

Rahul cut her off mid-sentence by kissing her thoroughly. Meghna met him halfway, revelling in the strength of his arms around her. She freed her hands to let them roam over the large expanse of his exposed chest, her fingers tangling in the dark silken hair. Rahul groaned against her lips, his body shuddering with the iron control he was imposing on it.

He caught hold of both her hands and held them down by her sides. Meghna opened her eyes to look at Rahul, ready to protest. When she met the ardent look of desire in his eyes, her lashes came down to cover the answering light in her own grey ones.

"Just give me a couple of minutes. Let me get some clothes on. Then we can go have breakfast."

"You look great just as you are," commented Meghna, looking at him boldly.

"Yeah, I know," said Rahul, completely audacious. "Only I don't want to embarrass the others."

"Such modesty," Meghna shook her head, giving him a mocking look, her eyes twinkling.

"Now are you turning away or should I…" Rahul's hand went to his waist to pull off his towel.

Meghna turned away in a hurry to hide her blushing face against the curtain.

"You may look now. I'm all done."

Meghna turned around to find Rahul dressed in figure hugging jeans and a black t-shirt, his feet bare. He stood before the mirror on the dressing table combing his hair. Meghna walked up to him and asked, "Are we going somewhere?"

"Not we. I am." Catching hold of the look of disappointment on Meghna's face, he elaborated, "I think you need to sleep for a few hours. I've a couple of jobs to finish in the meanwhile. I should be back," he lifted his left arm to look at the sleek watch on his wrist, "by two."

"Alone?" asked Meghna. Rahul looked at her strangely, not understanding. When he did, he gave her a broad smile before slipping an arm around

Meghna's shoulders and pulling her close. "Believe me," he bent down and whispered in her ear, "I'd much rather sleep with you. But I do have these errands to run. So, that's that." He shrugged his broad shoulders before dragging her out of the room. They had breakfast with Sanjay and Reema, the children having already had theirs. Sasha and Rehaan were absorbed in the Tom and Jerry cartoon show on TV.

"This *upma* and *chutney* are out of this world, *Bhabhi*; you've outdone yourself." Rahul praised enthusiastically as he served himself a second helping.

"Well, you'll have to tell Meghna that. She's the one who made the breakfast," confessed Reema.

Rahul looked at Meghna in amazement. He was reminded of the time she had insisted on making lunch for Sanjay and him. She had been experimenting her newly acquired culinary skills on them. The runny *dal*, misshapen, rubbery *rotis* and half-cooked rice flashed before his mind's eye. Rahul felt laughter bubble in his throat as he recalled the scene. Meeting his eyes, Meghna recollected the same incident. Only to Rahul's further surprise, instead of flashing thunder, her face settled into a smug expression, a look of confidence challenging him to withdraw his own compliment.

Rahul laid down his spoon before reaching for her right hand.

Her nerveless fingers dropped hers, the spoon clattering down noisily on the dining table. She raised shy eyes to look at the man she had fallen in love with.

Rahul raised her hand to his lips, turning it around, kissing her palm before closing her fingers over it. Meghna felt a thrill of pleasure when he said, "Excellent food. Thank you, honey."

Her eyes made a note of the tender light shining in his and she gave him a dazzling smile in response. "You're welcome."

They continued to eat their breakfast, seemingly unaware of the other two people sitting at the dining table.

Sanjay offered Rahul the keys to his Fortuner as the latter was donning his shoes.

"No, thanks, Sanjay. I'm taking Meghna's bike." Rahul showed him the keys that Meghna had given him earlier. He left the flat with a spring in his step. He wore a bright blue baseball cap over his dark, unruly locks. He sat astride the bike and stroked it lovingly, feeling close to its owner. Which was the reason why he opted to use it instead of the more comfortable four-wheeler.

His first stop was at a car rental agency to hire a Volkswagen Vento for the evening. He arranged with the man in charge to have it delivered at Kalpataru Residency in Sion by 5.30 pm.

Then he went to JW Marriot Hotel in Juhu and reserved a private dining room at their Saffron Restaurant. The room could comfortably seat twenty. Rahul explained to the manager exactly how he wanted the room decorated. He took his time going over the menu and carefully choosing the starters, the main course and the dessert, having an idea of Meghna's likes and dislikes. He finally ordered a bottle of champagne and left once both he and the manager came to an understanding.

His last stop was at the jewellers. He went to Tribovandas Zaveri at Opera House. He asked to see some rings. The salesman showed him a variety of diamond rings. Rahul studied them with great concentration but wasn't happy with any of them. He looked at the man behind the counter and asked, "Do you have anything else? I mean rings with other precious stones?"

"Yes sir," replied the salesman before having the diamond rings removed and bringing forth three more trays. They glittered with sapphires, emeralds, rubies, pearls, and corals. Rahul ran his index finger over them, looking totally uninspired by the lot.

On the third tray, he caught the flash of a large opal set in a cluster of small diamonds. "This is it," declared Rahul, his face alight with pleasure and satisfaction.

The salesman lifted the ring from the holder and wiping it with a piece of chamois leather, placed it on a tray covered with royal blue velvet cloth. It looked even more attractive against that background.

Rahul looked at the ring with enchantment. The opal appeared to blaze with a fire at its centre. It was oval in shape and glittered with a myriad of colours as Rahul lifted it in the palm of his hand and turned it towards the light. It reminded him of Meghna's eyes, flashing at every turn of her head.

Rahul looked at the salesman and said, "I need a size ten, please." The salesman nodded before checking the size. "Could you wait for about fifteen minutes, sir? We'll have it altered by then. Or do you want to come back later?" He asked respectfully, while handing over the ring to his assistant to have it modified.

"I'll wait. Or better yet, can you show me some earrings and pendant to match the ring? Oh, by the way, I will be paying in British pounds. Please make my bill accordingly."

The salesman beamed at Rahul before walking over to another cabinet to bring some earrings and necklaces to show his affluent client.

Rahul had never shopped for jewellery before. He realised he enjoyed buying things for Meghna. He would have preferred to have brought her along, but this evening was meant to be a surprise.

Rahul came down to earth as the salesman placed the various trays before him. He stared at them as the opals and diamonds winked at him under the bright overhead lights. He studied the trays, one by one, visualising Meghna in each set of jewellery.

Finally, he settled for earrings of exactly the same design as the ring; and a necklace to match. Well, the necklace was a beauty. The design was V-shaped with a large opal in the centre with matching pairs of opals on both sides, the stones diminishing in size as they moved to the ends of the two branches of the V. Thin gold chains at the two ends went around the nape. Each opal was surrounded by tiny sparkling diamonds which appeared to wink at Rahul.

He liked the vision of Meghna adorned in this particular piece. He nodded his head to the salesman and requested him to gift-wrap it.

"What about a bracelet, sir?" The smart salesman looked at his customer hopefully expecting to add some more commission to the fat one he must have already earned.

Rahul grinned at him and said, "Why not? I'm sure I can afford it. But don't show me too many. Just something to go with the necklace."

The salesman eagerly went to get the one piece he had in mind. He showed it to Rahul for approval. Rahul liked what he saw and asked the salesman to pack them all. "But pack the ring separately," he told him.

Rahul waited impatiently, tapping his shoe-clad feet on the plush carpet while the accountant prepared the bill. He ran a cursory glance over it before handing over the value in British currency. He added a generous tip in Indian rupees for the salesman. "For your excellent service," he smiled.

Rahul stepped out of the air-conditioned interior of the shop into the sunshine, a satisfied smile lurking on his lips. He was quite happy with the way the morning had worked out. Now he looked forward to the evening with great anticipation.

13

Meghna must have slept for barely half an hour when her cell buzzed on the side table. Normally, she wouldn't have kept her phone nearby during sleep. But she didn't want to miss in case Rahul called. In a state of half-sleep, she took the cell to check the caller ID and was irritated to see it was Prashant. She rejected the call and tried to get back to sleep again.

But Prashant was persistent. He called again and yet again. Meghna was fully awake now and remembering the sense of remorse she felt at using him the earlier night, took the call.

"Hello Prashant," she said, keeping the impatience out of her voice with great difficulty.

"Hi Meghna, are you still angry with me?" he asked in a small voice.

Meghna immediately felt contrite. She never wanted to demean him. After all, they had been teaching together for two years and meeting at least five days a week. It was a friendship of sorts and she didn't want to break it. All the advice Rahul had given her regarding Prashant went out of the window as Meghna replied in a gentle voice, "Of course not

Prashant. I only hope you aren't upset with me after last night. I didn't mean to be rude. But…"

"Prove it," he said, much to her amazement.

"Huh?" All trace of sleep had disappeared by now.

"I said *prove it*. Go out with me today evening. We'll have dinner at wherever you want to go," said Prashant, his voice suddenly oozing confidence.

What had she got herself into? And how to get out of this one? Meghna was confused, but just for a moment. "Prashant, we have guests at home." Her fingers crossed automatically at the white lie, "I won't be able to have dinner with you. I'm so sorry," she said, quite glad of the excuse.

"Then meet me now," insisted Prashant in a desperate voice. He needed to get her alone and soon. Otherwise, that gorilla from London will take her away permanently from him.

Meghna thought quickly. Rahul was out and probably will be for the next few hours. She thought it best to meet Prashant and explain to him where he stood. And she did owe him an apology that couldn't be made over the phone. "Okay," she said to Prashant's surprise. "Where?"

"Why don't you come over to my flat?" His mother was at work and he was all alone, having taken the day off. He was too disturbed after last night to be of much use at work.

Meghna didn't think twice before agreeing and took his address. It wasn't far, just at Dosti Apartments in Wadala. She quickly changed into jeans and t-shirt, combed her hair and left after calling out to Reema. With no bike, she took a cab to Prashant's apartment.

He opened the door even before she rang the bell. Meghna went in tentatively, guessing that he was alone. Her only confidence was that he was an old friend.

"Come in Meghna," said Prashant, feeling his chest swell with excitement. He finally had her alone. She had been playing fast and loose with him for two years, or so he believed. It didn't strike him that it was he who had been interested in having her for a girl friend while she had always considered him as only a friend.

He gestured to her to sit in the two-seater, hoping to be close to her. But Meghna pretended to not see it and settled down on the single sofa. The disappointed Prashant brought her a glass of water. "Late night or what? You look tired," he grinned stupidly, his eyes devouring her slim figure in the tight-fitting jeans and t-shirt.

She took a sip from the glass before keeping it on a side table and looked at him. "I'm terribly sorry about last night, Prashant. I hope I haven't hurt you," she apologised sincerely, her eyes compassionate as she looked at him. Deep down she knew that their friendship wasn't going to last.

Prashant shook his head even before she completed the sentence. "Of course not, Meghna. He's your guest and you had to take care of him. I understand that. You and I go a long way and I know that no one can come between us."

Now where the hell did that spring from? Meghna turned her startled gaze to his face and was shocked to see that he had stepped really close to her. "I don't understand what you mean," she said, her voice louder than before.

He sat on the arm of her sofa, his hand on her shoulder. "Come on Meghna. Don't tell me you aren't aware that I am in love with you." He pressed his hot lips against her cheek.

Meghna sprang from the sofa as if bitten, moving away from him even as she looked at him with shocked eyes. She hadn't expected this even if Rahul had warned her about Prashant's feelings for her. She shook her head in denial, rubbing away the sensation of his lips against her cheek with her left hand.

Prashant got up too and walked towards her. "Meghna, just give me some time and I will convince you that you love me too. We have spent two years together. Was there a choice?" Once again, he stepped too close for comfort.

Meghna felt like an idiot for having come to meet him at his home. She had to escape before he did something they both would regret.

"Prashant, tell you what? I'm too tired to think straight. Let me go back home and get some rest. Can we continue our talk tomorrow? I'll meet you again." She walked towards the door saying this, her fingers crossed again as she lied to him for the second time.

She was surprised and triumphant when Prashant let her go. But it had been too easy. She pulled the automatic lock on the front door and was shocked to find that it wouldn't budge. She was locked in the flat with Prashant. What the hell did he plan to do? She felt a powerful adrenalin rush as she turned her tempestuous face towards him, her grey eyes flaming with anger.

"Open the door, Prashant," she ordered, her voice soft and intense.

Prashant put both his hands up and said, "Chill Meghna. You came just now. What's the rush?" He took a step towards her.

She moved, her back pressed against the door, heart beating hard. What was he going to do?

"Let's have a drink together." He walked to the kitchen, confident that she had no way to escape.

Meghna desperately put her hand in her shoulder bag and speed-dialed Rahul's number on her cell, keeping an eye out for her tormentor, who returned with two beers before she could say anything. She slipped the phone back into her bag, keeping the line open, for Rahul to listen in when he took her call.

"Come Meghna," Prashant patted the two-seater again as he offered her a beer. Meghna looked at him warily, her whole body tense. This was not her dance partner of two years. He was a stranger. The other Prashant wouldn't have dared to keep her locked in. He was too faint-hearted or so she had believed.

"Come on Meghna," invited Prashant again, confident of having his way with her somehow or the other. "Have some beer and let's talk."

'Talk' sounded good and losing some of her fear, Meghna walked slowly towards the sofa. She again sat on the edge of the single seater and took the can of beer from him, making sure that their fingers didn't touch. She didn't much care for the smirk on Prashant's face as he said, "Cheers!" before taking a long swig from his can.

"Go on, you don't want it to get warm, do you?" he suggested courteously, his dark eyes watching her avidly.

Meghna was aware that the phone was on and she hoped Rahul was hearing their conversation. "Er… Prashant," her voice choked on his name as she felt a strong sense of revulsion. She cleared her throat before talking again, "Is this your own flat or have you rented it?" She opened the beer can and took a sip to wet her parched throat, her eyes not leaving his face, ready to pounce at the least movement.

Prashant frowned as if wondering why she was asking him such a question. "It's my own," he said, finishing his beer.

Meghna recoiled when he got up.

But he went to the kitchen to get himself another drink. How to bring the location of his flat into the dialogue without letting him know that she was feeding information to someone? She thought hard as he walked back to sit on the arm of her sofa yet again.

She pressed herself as far away from him as possible and asked, "Dosti is a good builder I've heard and this flat is fairly new. Have you always lived in Wadala?"

Prashant deliberately moved closer to remove the beer can from her trembling hand, without bothering to answer her. He placed both cans on a side table before sliding on to the sofa beside her. He had already finished his second beer, boosting his courage. When Meghna went to get up, he pulled her into his lap, his arms clamped tightly around her. Meghna let out a small scream before he pressed his hand over her mouth.

"Listen, I'm not going to harm you," he said. "There's no need to scream. I just want to love you." He pressed his lips to Meghna's throat as she squirmed, unable to get out of his hold. With great difficulty she released her arms and clawed at his hands. He let her go when the skin on the back of his hands burned from the cuts wielded by her sharp nails.

She jumped away from him the moment he moved his hands away.

Prashant was shocked as he studied the scratches on his hands. He looked up at her, anger in his eyes. "I told you I won't hurt you," he snarled, walking towards her.

Her grey eyes shimmered with unshed tears. Surely, he wasn't going to rape her, was he? She shook her head from side to side, keen to avoid him. But there was nowhere to run—just the hall and kitchen with no door in-between. She was once again pressed against the front door, willing it to open.

The bell rang as if on cue and Prashant cursed, virulently. Who the hell was it at this time of the afternoon? He wasn't expecting anybody.

Rahul had been driving home to Sion when Meghna called. He switched on his bluetooth and was shocked to hear her talking to Prashant of all people. He pulled to the side of the road and stopped the bike. He took his cell phone out of his pocket and checked the location of Meghna's mobile on the GPS.

She wasn't far, just a few minutes away and thank God for that.

Rahul gunned the bike towards Dosti Apartments in Wadala and reached Prashant's flat just as he heard the other man say, "I told you I won't hurt you." Rahul felt violent as he rang the doorbell long and hard.

The moment the door opened, Rahul put his shoe-clad foot in the doorway, not keen to have the door close in his face. He glared at Prashant and asked, "Where's Meghna?" He couldn't see Prashant's hand pressed against her throat as he held her against the wall. Rahul heard a gagging sound and immediately pushed the other man out of his way as he walked into the flat.

Meghna was pressed against the wall near the door, tears running down her cheeks as she massaged her bruised neck. Her lips moved soundlessly as she fell into Rahul's arms, so relieved to see him.

Rahul just about managed to see the fist coming in his direction as he turned with Meghna in his arms. He caught Prashant's fist quite easily in his left hand and twisted it, hard. He lifted his right arm and slapped the other man hard on his cheek. Prashant reeled at the hard slap and held his cheek with both hands, his eyes glaring hatred at Rahul.

Rahul thrust his face close to his adversary and snapped, "Just stay away from Meghna," his honey-gold eyes promising murder otherwise.

Was she glad that Rahul had arrived in the nick of time! He held Meghna close as they walked out of the flat, neither of them saying a word. She was just glad that he had arrived in time. But he was having a difficult time holding on to his temper as he had a good mind to put her over his knee and give her a sound thrashing for her irresponsible behaviour. Why the hell did she have to visit Prashant at his home of all places?

Rahul stopped the bike near Meghna's building and waited for her to get off before driving away, not uttering a single word; not keen to say something he was bound to regret.

eghna was shocked by Rahul's behaviour, to the point that she almost forgot the trauma she had undergone at Prashant's hands. What was with the man? Why the hell did he go away without uttering a word? She had been sure he would hug and comfort her in the privacy of her room. But… but he had just ridden away. Did he care for her at all? What could be more important right now?

She went up to her flat, her face pale. She walked to her room without meeting the other members of the family and was shocked to see the bruise marks on her throat where Prashant had held her.

She rushed to the bathroom and threw up. Her whole system was shaken by the incident and Rahul's subsequent behaviour hadn't helped. Controlling the tears that were fighting to spill over, Meghna stood under the shower for a long time, scrubbing away Prashant's touch.

She wore a sleeveless tee with a turtleneck to cover her bruises and went to find the others. Rahul was still not home and he wasn't picking her calls. She had called him at least five times, and she decided not to call him again.

The kids had already had lunch and were having their nap. She sat at the dining table with Sanjay and Reema without talking much. After a couple of attempts, the two of them continued to converse between themselves, leaving her alone. No one spoke about Rahul, much to Meghna's anger and disappointment. She broke the *naan* into pieces and kept moving them around in her plate, her appetite non-existent. After a while, she excused herself to go to her bedroom. Sleep eluded her as she oscillated between hurt and anger. She added 'abominable' to the adjectives she used for Rahul.

The subject of her thoughts had gone to a bar and sloshed himself silly. He didn't want to answer Meghna's calls as he wasn't sure what he wanted to tell her. She was an adult and it wasn't up to him to teach her how to live. But that didn't stop him from being angry with her. He messaged Sanjay that he would be out for the day so that they didn't wait lunch for him.

The first thing Rahul did after leaving Meghna was to postpone his dinner plans at JW Marriott for the evening. It was not the right time to bare his heart to his lady love. He wondered whether the time will ever be right as his anger mounted a few more notches as he recalled Meghna's behaviour that afternoon. He had already warned her about Prashant's feelings towards her. Despite that, she had flirted with the man last night and had the nerve to visit him today at his flat. Did she have no sense? Not for a minute did Rahul believe that she might be attracted to Prashant.

He was quite confident that Meghna loved himself and none else. He had driven away as he felt violent and hadn't wanted to do something that he would regret for life.

He had ridden all the way to Colaba to Leopold Café and set out to drink himself under the table. He ordered some food after downing four large pegs of whiskey. All the temper in the world hadn't spoilt his appetite and he had a hearty lunch. It was almost four when Rahul got on his bike to go to Chowpatty and walked on the seashore. The waves had a calming effect on him and after a couple of hours, he left to go back home.

Meghna and Rahul managed to ignore each other during the rest of the day. The other couple stuck to an inane conversation after taking a look at their stony expressions.

All hell broke loose that night. Everyone had settled for the night while Meghna sat brooding in her room. She couldn't sleep and she decided she wouldn't let Rahul sleep peacefully either.

She got up immediately to put her thought into action and went to his room. She knocked and waited for him to open the door. He scowled heavily when he saw who it was. Refusing to be cowed down, she walked in jauntily. Placing her hands on her hips, she glared at him. That's when she noticed that he was in his boxers and she had a tough time not running away from his room.

Rahul's eyebrows touched his hairline in enquiry. He still didn't utter a word.

"What's with the silent treatment?" she asked, her voice trembling with emotion.

"When my words have no value, it makes sense to keep quiet, doesn't it?" he came back with a question of his own.

Her grey eyes shimmered with unshed tears. "You can't do this to me, Rahul. Prashant's a bastard and it was a traumatic experience. You weren't even there for me after that," she accused.

"I was there when you needed me, right?"

"No. You left me and went away." She had so wanted to be held in his strong arms to feel safe. But he had gone away. She refused to let the tears flow, not keen to let him see her weakness.

"What would you've had me do? It was easy to knock sense into Prashant with a hard slap. But you?" he asked, refusing to be moved by her damp eyes.

"How dare you?" she snarled. "How dare you compare me with Prashant? Yesterday, I was in a situation and yes, you did come to my rescue. Don't you care enough about me to help me get over the ordeal? Believe me, it was a horrible experience," she yelled now.

"And one that you brought on yourself," he said cruelly.

Meghna's jaw fell open, shock on her face. She turned away from him, hugging herself protectively, her eyes completely dry by now.

Rahul looked at her dejected figure and felt sorry for her. Now that he was calmer, he was ready to meet her halfway. His intention hadn't been to hurt her. He had needed to cool down before confronting her and that was the reason he had gone away. But she was still on her high horse. He walked up to her and placed a hand on her slumped shoulder. "Meghna."

She didn't respond, still very hurt and angry. He put his arms around her and hugged her lightly. He adored her and couldn't see her hurt.

"I'm sorry, honey! I am truly sorry. My only excuse is my jealousy. I…"

"What?" Meghna twisted around in his arms to stare at him, her eyes wide with astonishment. "Jealous? Of what? Who?" She shook her head in a daze. "Don't tell me you are jealous of Prashant?"

Rahul grimaced, shrugging. "Well, he has been spending a lot of time with you in the past two years. While I've been missing in action…"

She punched him on his shoulder. "And who's fault is that?" Her heart soared, all her hurt wiped away in a single sweep. Rahul was jealous of Prashant of all people in the world. It was an effort not to giggle as she felt a heady sense of excitement. It could mean only one thing. That he loved her, a lot.

Rahul laughed, so glad that Meghna wasn't upset any longer. "I know. Will you forgive me?"

"There's nothing to forgive." She nestled against his shoulder, wrapping her arms around his waist. "And I'm sorry. I should have heeded your warning about Prashant being interested in me more than as a friend." She moved back to gaze into Rahul's honey brown eyes, smiling when she saw the tenderness in them. "I don't know why he thought there was more to our friendship."

Rahul shook his head, kissing her forehead. "I wonder what you really see when you look at yourself in a mirror? Unless… let me see. I suppose you take your gorgeous appearance for granted. But we guys tend to have a different perception, you know. We think…"

She placed a hand over his mouth, shaking her head at him. "I want to only know what you think. I'm not interested in any other man's opinion."

And he told her, whispering all the thoughts which kept him awake at night, all because of her.

15

Post lunch the next day, Meghna was sitting comfortably on Rahul's lap as they snuggled together on his bed, reading from their respective books. She gave a sigh of pleasure as she stretched, raising her arms behind to put them around his neck. Rahul's mystery novel fell to the floor with a thud when he turned her around to kiss her hungrily.

They slid down on the bed to lie together spoon fashion, Rahul holding her close. "I'm going to have a brief shut-eye," said Meghna, yawning. She had barely slept the earlier night.

It was much later at five pm when he ran a hand through her hair, shaking her gently, "Wake up, sleepyhead."

Meghna gave him a sweet smile, her eyes still sleepy as she wound her arms around his neck.

"I was dreaming about you. I wonder whether you're real." She spoke softly, not properly awake yet.

"Let me show you," growled Rahul before bending down and nipping her lower lip sharply.

"Ouch!"

Rahul smothered the muffled cry by kissing Meghna firmly on her lips.

She returned his kiss with equal fervour.

He raised his head to look at her flushed face. "It's time for you to be up. I'm taking you out for the evening."

Meghna smiled at him curiously before asking, "Where?"

Rahul shook his head saying, "You'll find out when we get there."

Which only made her more inquisitive. "You never did say where you went the other day."

Rahul looked at her with a teasing smile on his lips. "Now that'd be telling, wouldn't it?" He shook his head. "Get up, lazybones, and get ready fast. I don't want to be late. We've an appointment at 6.30."

Meghna pouted at him as she rightly concluded that she wouldn't be able to elicit anything from him. She felt a spark of excitement shoot through her system like a bolt of electricity as she met Rahul's honey gold gaze, which was full of promises. "What should I wear?" she asked.

"Hmm..." Rahul looked at her thoughtfully. "Something formal should be fine." He bent closer and whispered in her ear, "You look sexy in anything and everything." He enjoyed the way the colour rushed to her face, her grey eyes sparkling. He pulled her out of the bed and giving her a slap on her bottom, said, "Get moving, woman. I don't have all the time in the world."

"Ooo..." shrieked Meghna, rubbing a hand over her behind. She gave Rahul a mock glare, saying, "That hurt, you big oaf."

"Oh, really," Rahul widened his eyes mischievously, moving towards her and pulling her into his arms, caressing her damaged flesh with both his hands. "There, does that feel okay or should I kiss it better?" he asked teasingly.

Meghna raised her startled gaze to his, panic in her grey eyes. "No, no, I'm fine," she said hastily before stepping out of his arms and rushing into the bathroom, his amused laughter following her.

When she stepped out after about half-an-hour and a relaxed bath, there was no sign of her tormentor. She walked to her wardrobe and threw the door open to run a finger through all the dresses hanging there.

Meghna quickly settled on a turquoise blue, full length dress of crepe. Pulling it off the hanger, she placed it on the bed. She hunted in the side cupboard for matching shoes and clutch. The hidden locker in her cupboard contained a set of turquoise jewellery which she placed on her dressing table. After getting all the accessories together, she set to work on her appearance.

She piled her hair on the top of her head and set it in place with a pair of silver combs. She left some tendrils hanging loose on both sides of her face. She wore very light makeup. Blue eye shadow with dark brown eyeliner outlining her large eyes gave a mysterious depth to the grey eyes. A light golden brown on her cheekbones before applying a coat of powder enhanced the shape of her firm jaw line. Her naturally long eyelashes defied the need for mascara. She applied a dark pinkish mauve shade of lipstick, the colour of wild orchids. She gave her face a once over in the mirror. Her eyes were shining with anticipation and she smiled at her image before nodding in approval.

She slipped on a strapless bra and matching lace panties before donning the blue dress over her head and pulling it over the length of her body to fall down to her bare feet. The crepe silk rustled and caressed as she moved. The thin shoe-string straps displayed her slim shoulders to advantage, her dusky skin glowing golden in the artificial light above the dressing table.

She clipped long earrings to her earlobes. They almost touched her shoulders, a string of turquoise and silver beads, alternately strung on silver wire.

A rope of the same beads decorated her slender neck while a matching armlet graced her right arm. She stepped into the high-heeled shoes in the same shade of blue as her dress. Transferring a tube of lipstick, house keys and some tissues into the silver clutch, she closed it with a snap. Applying some perfume, she left her room with a lilt in her step. It was 5.30 and she was bang on time.

Rahul was waiting for her in the hall, nursing a glass of iced tea in his hand. The others were nowhere in sight.

"They've all gone out to watch a film." Rahul answered the unspoken question in her grey eyes, his own travelling hungrily over her. He didn't utter a single word as he absorbed her elegant appearance. Words seemed too mundane to describe the feelings she aroused in him.

Meghna ran her gaze quickly from the top of his sleek dark head to the well polished black leather shoes adorning his feet. He looked too handsome to be let loose. He wore formal black pants and a crisp white dressy shirt with a black bow tie. He lifted a black dinner jacket and held it over his shoulder by the crook of one finger when he saw that she was fully ready.

The excitement that had been playing football in her stomach increased manifold and rose to become stuck in her throat, making it impossible for her to utter a word. She looked at him wordlessly, her eyes saying it all as they met the answering fire in his gaze.

Rahul offered her his arm. She placed a trembling hand in the crook of his elbow and the two of them stepped out of the flat together. Much to her disappointment, he refused to meet her eyes on their way down.

Meghna took a step towards the gate as she presumed that they would leave the compound and hail a passing cab.

Rahul's restraining hand on her arm stopped her from walking further. He silently turned her towards the navy-blue Volkswagen Vento parked on the left side. A driver had turned up earlier at the flat to leave the keys with him.

Rahul opened the passenger door for Meghna, still without uttering a word. That was something new, a tongue-tied Rahul. *Wonders will never cease,* thought Meghna, a trifle grim at his silence. Once again, all her efforts at dressing up seemed to have gone waste. She took cheer from the thought that the last time it had improved after a while. She gave a surreptitious glance at her companion's attractive profile and wondered at his tense jaw when he settled behind the wheel.

"Rahul," she called out hesitantly, her eyes pleading.

He turned to look at her, his golden eyes blazing with desire, sending a bolt of lightning through Meghna's nerves.

Rahul had read her expression correctly as he raised her right hand to his lips, his eyes holding her turbulent gaze. "We'd have never left the flat if I'd started to tell you how ravishing you look," he drawled, his sexy voice low.

Meghna blushed rosily as she looked at him shyly.

"What, no come back? I can't believe it," teased Rahul, laughter in his eyes as he looked at her blushing face.

"I wouldn't have minded not leaving the flat," came the soft but firm response as Meghna finally found her voice.

"Oh?" Rahul's eyebrows met his hairline. "That would've put to waste all my efforts. And to tell you the truth," he added, tongue-in-cheek, "I wouldn't have felt safe in the flat with you, the two of us alone. I'm not sure what you'd do..."

Meghna stopped the teasing words by reaching over to press her mouth to his, inviting his kiss. Rahul obliged her delightfully and silence reigned in the air-conditioned interior of the car for the next few minutes.

He lifted his head to look down at her. "You look wonderful. Good enough to eat," he whispered, his fingers playing with the tendrils of hair dancing tantalisingly about her face.

"You too, you handsome hunk. I'm scared of the women we might be meeting during the course of the evening. I'll have a tough time protecting your honour," she pulled his leg, and was thrilled to watch the ruddy colour seeping into his face at her wholesome compliment.

"How safe am I from present company?" he countered.

"Mmm…" Meghna pretended to think hard. "That depends on how well you treat me, you know. If you please me well enough with adoring kisses from time to time, I might consider not laying a finger on your honour…"

Rahul's roar of mirth filled the car even as Meghna's tinkling laughter joined in. He put the car into forward gear and drove through the gates, chuckling under his breath. The atmosphere was light as they travelled along with the home going traffic, heading towards Juhu.

"Where're we going?" asked Meghna once again.

Rahul shook his head and said, "Wait and see."

Meghna's eyes rounded in astonishment and delight as they entered the gates of the JW Marriott Hotel and climbed over the inclined drive to the front entrance.

A valet came forward and opened the passenger door before saluting smartly. Meghna stepped out of the car and looked around her in awe, taking in the surroundings as she waited for Rahul to join her. He handed the keys to the valet before offering his arm to her once more. He had worn his jacket before stepping out of the car and Meghna felt proud of her handsome escort.

Rahul raised his brow enquiringly, waiting for her comment.

"This is wonderful," came the breathless praise. "Thank you, darling Rahul, I've never been here before."

"I know," replied Rahul, his voice equally soft, as he escorted her through the glass doors into the air-conditioned lobby.

Meghna felt torn as she tried to take in her surroundings while she didn't want to take her eyes off Rahul.

They walked across the length of the lobby and went down the curving staircase to the right. When they reached the lower level, Rahul directed her towards the door on the right leading to the Saffron Restaurant.

They walked between the neat rows of tables to reach a door on the opposite end of the wall. Meghna felt curiouser and curiouser like Alice in Wonderland. The manager opened the door with a flourish as Rahul allowed her to precede him.

Meghna's gasp of delight was barely audible. But Rahul heard it as the manager closed the door behind the two of them.

She wouldn't have recognised the room even if she had seen it before today. Gone were the long conference table and many chairs. The room was large with just the one table for two, set at the left corner of the room away from the entrance. Meghna's feet sank into the plush carpet beneath her feet as she stepped forward, her gaze flitting about her in admiration.

The only light came from the twelve fat, aromatic candles set in the two branches of candelabra standing on the floor, on both sides of the table. Large, comfortable chairs with cushions were placed facing each other across the table. AR Rahman's music played softly in the background.

There was a bottle of champagne chilling out in a bucket of ice on a side table. The whole ambience was one of celebration. What really hit her eye were the flowers. There were flowers placed in ceramic bowls, vases and pots of various shapes and sizes on every available surface in the room. A centrepiece of red roses in a wide bowl decorated the dining table. There were anthuriums, roses and asters flanked by gladioli, baby's breath and golden lawn. Meghna's eyes opened wide with pleasure as she moved closer to the bowl of anthuriums to touch the waxy petals to find for herself if they were real. She had never seen so many flowers together under one roof—not even in a flower shop.

She turned glittering eyes towards the man who was obviously responsible for all this extravagance. She put out both her hands to him and said, "Rahul," her voice no more than a hushed murmur. She cleared her throat delicately before continuing, "Rahul, I'm overwhelmed. I'm so thrilled that I don't know what to say. Thank you." She walked closer to him in response to the tug from his fingers and kissed him sweetly on his cheek. "Thank you, dear Rahul. This is all so awesome."

"I'm glad," came the hoarse response as Rahul pulled her into his arms.

"You must've gone to a whole lot of trouble and expense, Rahul," protested Meghna, feeling a mite guilty.

"You're worth all of this and more, honey," said Rahul, his teasing voice serious for a change. He bent down and captured her mouth in an adoring kiss, before lifting his dark head to meet her shining eyes and giving her a dazzling smile.

"I love you, Meghna darling. I always have. And now finally the hour of surrender has come. I'd be extremely happy to spend the rest of my life with you. Will you do me the honour of becoming my wife? Will you marry me? Please."

Meghna stared at Rahul with unblinking eyes. She couldn't believe her ears. She had had an inkling that he would ask her to marry him. But this abject surrender? More than that, the look of uncertainty lurking at the back of his eyes? She hadn't expected either. She shook her head delicately to clear it and was sorry to be the cause for the alarm in his eyes. She spoke in a rush to put him out of his misery. "Rahul!" Her voice was a throaty whisper as her arms went around his neck to cling to him, her soft body pressing close to his hard frame. "I love you too. And I'd be delighted to marry you. Yes, yes, yes, yes, and yes."

Rahul swooped down to smother her lips in a demanding kiss as his body shuddered in reaction. He had been almost sure of her response but somewhere deep down there had been a niggling doubt. The relief was just too great. He didn't want to stop kissing Meghna. He pressed his lips against her cheek and blazed a trail to her bare shoulder. "Meghna, I love you so. I just can't imagine how I spent all my life without you."

"Rahul," Meghna sighed happily. "I just can't believe that you love me, finally. All the years of waiting," she sighed. "Please tell me that it's not just wishful thinking on my part," she pleaded.

Rahul found her lips again and gave her a deep, soul-searing kiss. His tongue danced a tango with hers and both were gasping for breath as they came up for air.

"Did that feel real enough?" asked Rahul, his smile gentle as he studied her flushed face and red lips in the light of the candles.

"Yes," grinned Meghna, ear-to-ear. "But there's this small doubt. Do you think you can give a repeat performance, just so that…"

Rahul didn't wait for her to complete the sentence; obliging her with alacrity. "You look beautiful in that outfit. Extremely sexy, in fact. Marry me soon," he ordered. "I can't handle too many of these cold showers I've been taking from the time I arrived in Mumbai."

Meghna blushed delicately on hearing his passionate words, her eyes shining like stars. Looking at them, Rahul remembered the jewellery box he had carefully placed in his jacket pocket. He put his hand in and pulled the ring box out and drew Meghna's attention to it.

"Is that for me?" asked Meghna excitedly.

"That's right," said Rahul, waiting eagerly for her to open it.

Meghna pressed the catch and the lid sprang open. Her breath came in a rush, her lips parting in a tingle of excitement as she viewed the opal ring lying on the bed of velvet.

"But Rahul, this is superb," she said. "I've never come across anything so beautiful."

"I'm so pleased to hear that. Now, show me your left hand." Rahul lifted the ring from the box and raising her hand, slipped it on her slender ring finger. It was a perfect fit. He gave her a grin as he lifted her hand to his lips and kissed it lovingly. "There, now you're officially my fiancée."

Meghna drew her left hand which was still lying in his grasp to herself to admire the ring. The opal glittered extra bright in the candlelight. "Rahul, thank you." So saying, she kissed him at the corner of his lips. Her face suddenly puckered in a frown. "But I don't have anything to give you." There was disappointment in her voice.

"Says who? You have given me a positive reply to my proposal which is the best possible gift. What more can I ask for?" said Rahul, brushing his fingers over her forehead to remove the frown.

Meghna hugged him close, feeling contented with his reply.

"Now come on. Let's have some champagne and starters. You must be hungry." He led her towards the chair, holding her close to his side. He guffawed as her stomach grumbled loudly, as if on cue. He gently pushed her down on a chair before pressing a switch on the wall closest to him, which rang a bell at the serving station.

Soon, a waiter walked in with a tray containing a plate of *paneer chilli* and another of *tandoori chicken kebabs*. He placed them on the table before opening the bottle of chilled champagne and pouring the sparkling wine into two tall fluted glasses. Rahul waved him away when he offered to serve them.

"This looks delicious," exclaimed Meghna, staring at her brand-new fiancé with love shining in her eyes.

Rahul lifted a piece of *paneer* on a fork and offered it to her. He held her gaze pinned with his as he fed her slowly, patiently waiting for her to sip on her champagne in between. The music had now switched to *gazals* by Hariharan.

"Hey! I like that music a lot," said Meghna.

"I remember how you used to play his cassette until you wore out the ribbons," teased Rahul gently as he bit into the kebab Meghna offered him.

She fed him with her hand, enjoying the sensation of his tongue flicking over the tips of her fingers in a quick caress as he held her hand steady to his mouth. He remembered! Rahul recalled a whole lot of things from their younger days. She found that truly incredible. Meghna thought that she had been the only one mooning about her love in these past years when they had completely lost contact. The sense of having found a kindred spirit grew by the second.

They talked about everything under the sun, recollecting many incidents from Meghna's childhood. They also discussed their forthcoming wedding.

"I hope you don't want too elaborate an affair," said Rahul, looking at Meghna with anxiety in his golden-brown eyes.

Meghna was puzzled to see the look of worry on his face. "Why, Rahul?"

"Well, to tell you the truth, I don't think I can deny you anything, honey. So, if you want a big wedding with all the trimmings, well, so be it." He shrugged his broad shoulders philosophically, looking pretty unhappy.

"But?" prompted Meghna.

Rahul sighed, looking uncomfortable. *"Jaane do,* Meghna. Let's have a big wedding." He had the look of a lamb being led to the slaughter.

Meghna stifled the hysterical giggle which rose in her throat and fixed him with a glare. "I've just agreed to marry you, Rahul. And marriage to me means being truthful to each other; trusting and respecting one another's feelings." She paused, expecting him to say something.

He looked at her with a small frown marring his perfect features, waiting for her to continue.

"So why don't you begin to trust me and tell me what exactly is bothering you about having a big wedding?"

"Well," Rahul burst out. "I can't stand that kind of a horse circus, for one thing." He pulled at his bow tie to loosen it, as though the very thought of a big wedding had the power to strangle him.

He looked at her, his eyes beseeching. "Ideally, I'd like to elope. Least tension and the fastest way to tie the knot." He gave her a weak grin, realising that she didn't find the matter funny at all. "But I suppose Sanjay and Reema *Bhabhi* will never forgive me."

"Rahul…"

"Wait," Rahul put his hand up to stop her from interrupting. "I'm not even considering it."

"Liar."

"Meghna," protested Rahul. But his eyes gave him away. He continued, "Anyway, I suppose it's not worth considering." He gave her a hopeful look as he said it, only to receive a firm shake of Meghna's pretty head in response.

"Where's the need to elope, Rahul? It's not as though either of our family members will refuse to accept our marriage. So why bother to run away?" Meghna was genuinely perplexed.

The woman from Venus couldn't quite comprehend the kind of dread this male specimen from Mars was suffering from.

Just the thought of sitting through an elaborate Hindu wedding ceremony amidst a large crowd of friends and relatives made Rahul feel claustrophobic. He was almost tempted to withdraw his marriage proposal.

While Meghna couldn't see anything strange or frightening in undergoing such a ritual since it happened to her friends and relatives all the time.

They seemed to have reached a dead end with nowhere to turn. They stared at each other, trying to fathom how far the other would be ready to give in. Their first impasse as a couple and their married life had not even begun.

Rahul sighed dramatically as he spoke in a tone of abject sacrifice, "Why can't we have a small ceremony in your house with your immediate family and my father?" He didn't care to even mention his mother. "And say, a few close friends, limiting the number of guests to about twenty or so." He warmed to the subject as he found the idea thoroughly acceptable. He looked at his fiancée enquiringly, trying to gauge her reaction to this.

Meghna nodded her head slowly. "Yeah," she drew out the word. "I think that should be fine."

Rahul jumped up from his chair to pull her into his arms. "Let's seal the pact," he said before kissing her thoroughly. He felt such a wave of relief at what he thought was a lucky escape from a close shave. "You'll never regret this, Meghna honey," he promised in a hoarse voice, the moment they came up for air.

They continued to discuss the rest of the arrangements for the wedding. Dinner was served, only neither of them was exactly aware of what they ate as they were too absorbed in each other.

Rahul told her about the plan he had of shifting into his own apartment in London for the immediate future. "Later on, we can buy a house with a big garden, say within six months or so. We could do the house hunting together. That should be great fun." Rahul's eyes crinkled with an affectionate smile as he looked at Meghna's animated face as she hung on to his every word.

"Will it be possible to continue conducting dance classes there, do you think?" She asked him a trifle apprehensively.

"Why ever not? You can join any number of Dance Academies as a teacher with the kind of experience you have. That way you'll be able to make contacts and later on branch out on your own, when we shift to the larger house."

"Life must be quite expensive there, Rahul. Or that's what I've heard. Do you think I should maybe take up a regular job to help you with the finances? I don't want you to be burdened too much," offered Meghna, hesitating to ask him outright about the state of his wealth.

Rahul lifted her hand to his lips and kissing her palm, said, "Thanks, honey. But no, thanks. Just relax. You're marrying someone who's a billionaire a couple of times over," he said in a quiet, matter-of-fact tone. He looked at Meghna lovingly. Sweet, sensitive young thing. Not a greedy bone in her delectable body. He loved her all the more for it.

The topic changed to the Indians living in London and how Rahul passed his free time. He told her about his friends. Time flew by and looking at his watch Rahul saw that it was past eleven.

"Time to go home, honey. We must break the good news to Sanjay and Reema *Bhabhi!* I wonder if they'll be awake," said Rahul.

"Sanjay must've left for his flight to Dubai. Anyway, they both have an idea that you might pop the question."

"Very sure of me, were you?" A black eyebrow went up as Rahul ran a caressing finger down her petal soft cheek.

Hot colour suffused her face as Meghna met his twinkling glance shyly to nod her head truthfully.

"Lucky lady." Rahul hugged her close. "I was on tenterhooks until you said yes."

"Serve you right. You're too sure of yourself otherwise," came the pert rejoinder.

He grinned down at her. "I asked for that, I suppose. Although I don't find you lacking in confidence."

"Not now, may be. But the day you arrived and the next, you drove me crazy with your teasing ways. I was a nervous wreck. It was like meeting a stranger who had been too familiar in my dreams over the past six years. Bloody confusing," she bit out.

Rahul's grin widened, unabashed. "It's such fun getting a raise out of you, as you're too quick to jump to the bait." Meghna wrinkled her nose at him. "I don't plan to stop teasing you, ever. Don't even imagine that I'm going to change just because I'm crazily in love with you." He kissed her as if he couldn't stop himself.

Meghna wrapped her arms tightly around him before pressing her lips against his jaw line. "I wouldn't have you any other way. And I know how to stop you if you get to be too much," she paused dramatically.

"How?" Rahul glanced at her curiously. Her eyes glowed in the candlelight, shining with love and a trace of mischief.

"Like this." Meghna pressed her mouth to his.

"I like that," said Rahul, as they came up for air. "I think I should get to be *too much* as often as I can." He grinned at her as they moved forward to step into the outside world.

Meghna pressed herself close to her fiancé's taut body and said, "Thank you, Rahul, for a wonderful and memorable evening. I love you."

"Temptress," growled Rahul, curbing his desires out of respect to the still crowded restaurant. "Wait till we get home."

"Promises, promises," teased Meghna, taking a leaf out of his book. "Let's get home fast, then."

Rahul resisted the impulse to kiss her then and there and walked outside quickly, her hand tucked in his. The valet brought their car to the front door and Rahul got into the driver's seat after seeing Meghna into the passenger side.

Meghna leaned her head against his shoulder as he drove out of the hotel's gate. She gave a sigh of contentment as soft music washed over them from the car deck.

"Sleepy?" enquired Rahul, taking his eyes off the road for a moment to look at her face.

"No, not at all. I feel wide awake."

"Good, as the party is to continue when we get home," said Rahul.

Meghna turned her head to kiss him on his lean cheek. Her pink tongue darted out to caress him for a second. Rahul's hands trembled on the wheel as he fought for control. He moved to the left side of the road to stop the car, switching on the parking lights.

He pulled Meghna into his arms to give her a hard kiss. "Keep your hands to yourself if you want to reach home safely," he threatened her—half-playful, half-serious.

"But my hands are with me. I didn't even touch you." Meghna's eyes widened innocently.

"Very funny." Rahul looked at the woman who held him in the palm of her hand. He was ready to do just about anything for her. "Please, honey. I'm serious. I can't concentrate on my driving when you're pressed so close to me. I'm sure you understand." Rahul hated the thought of not being in control.

"Let me see," Meghna tilted her head to one side before looking at him from the corner of her eyes. "What're you ready to give me for not disturbing you?" she challenged.

"What do you want?" Rahul joined her in her flirtatious mood.

"Mmm…" she looked at him thoughtfully. "A couple of pieces of your clothing?" she asked.

Rahul gave her a startled glance before a grin split his face. "Of your choice or mine?" he asked cheekily.

Panic flared in her grey eyes. "I'll choose," she said in a rush.

"Okay, tell me," he laughed.

"Your bow tie and jacket," chose Meghna promptly.

"Anything to oblige you, sweetheart," said Rahul prior to removing the two garments and handing them over to his fiancée. "Will that be all?" he asked her.

"Not quite," Meghna moved close to him and opened the top two buttons of his shirt before pressing her lips to the strong column of his brown throat. "Mmm… I've been dying to do that throughout the evening."

It took Rahul all of a minute to bring a semblance of control to his surging emotions as he felt Meghna's lips against his skin. He cleared his throat before talking to her in a hoarse voice, "You should've told me earlier. Anything for you, love."

"Anything?" she fluttered her lashes at him.

What have I unleashed? wondered Rahul. He grinned at her as he realised that their engagement had improved her confidence tremendously. She was always forward in expressing her feelings. Lately, she had become unsure of him. Hence the unusual display of shyness. Now that she was sure of him, she had changed back to her original impish self, he surmised, thrilled with the result.

ahul took the key to the flat from Meghna. He lifted the fingers of her right hand in his left before raising it to his lips. He looked deeply into her eyes and said, "Love you, honey."

Meghna met his honey gold gaze head on, her own stormy grey eyes blazing with love, "I love you too, Rahul."

Rahul pulled her close to his side as he opened the door to the flat.

What happened next seemed to unfold in slow motion. The whole scene was etched in Meghna's mind for ever.

The lights were ablaze in the hall as Reema got up from her seat on hearing the key in the lock. Meghna let go of Rahul's hand to rush towards her *bhabhi* to share her good news.

Just when she had taken a couple of steps, she felt the presence of another person in the same room as she caught the image of a woman in her peripheral.

It was a strange woman, probably in her late twenties. Meghna stopped in her tracks, wondering who could be visiting so late in the night. The guest was dressed in a short black dress; her lips, a slash of scarlet. Meghna wondered at the terrible anger that burned in the other woman's gaze as she looked at the younger woman who had walked in on Rahul's arm. The next moment the newcomer turned towards Meghna's fiancé.

"Rahul," she purred, both her arms outstretched in greeting as she moved towards him.

"What in the blazes…?" bit out Rahul before his lips were smothered in a possessive kiss.

He put his hands on Aisha's shoulders to push her away in disgust. *What the hell was this specimen doing in India, that too in Sanjay's home?* he wondered.

"Darling Rahul," continued Aisha relentlessly, seemingly oblivious to the temper sparking in Rahul's eyes. "I missed you so," she drawled. "Rajni Aunty assured me that you must also be missing me. I'm so glad of this chance to surprise you…"

Meghna didn't stop to hear any more. The whole world had come crashing down her ears. Feeling numb with shock, she rushed to her room, not heeding Rahul's "Meghna, wait."

"Rahul, let the poor girl go. She'll never be able to make you as happy as I can. She appears rather immature, you know," Aisha continued to purr in his ear, her fingers thrust into his hair, caressing his scalp.

Rahul felt torn. He wanted to rush to Meghna to reassure her. At the same time, he wanted this thorn-in-the-flesh out of Sanjay's flat first thing.

He scowled down at Aisha before thrusting her away completely. "Just shuddup, won't you?" he snarled impatiently, uncaring that he was being rude.

He turned his disturbed gaze to Reema. "*Bhabhi,* let me drop Aisha at her hotel. In the meanwhile," his eyes were pleading, "take care of Meghna for me, please?"

Reema nodded, trusting her instincts. She had been shocked to find Aisha at their doorstep an hour ago, claiming to be Rahul's betrothed. Although Reema had been desperate to call her bluff, she hadn't been sure enough about Rahul to throw out someone who was obviously aware of where he was staying in Mumbai. Reema had concluded that Aisha must be very sure of his affection, as she had come to meet him, all the way from London. Well, now things were obviously turning for the better. Rahul was not at all happy to see this Aisha. Quite the opposite, it appeared.

Rahul lifted the single piece of luggage Aisha had with her and left the flat with her without uttering another word.

Reema went to Meghna's bedroom to find the door locked.

"Meghna," called out Reema as she knocked on her door.

"Is that you, Reema *Bhabhi*?" came the muffled response. "What's it, *Bhabhi*? I'm changing."

"Nothing, dear. Just wanted to check that you are okay. Rahul's gone to drop Aisha at her hotel."

And probably stay back the night, thought Meghna viciously. She felt awfully hurt and upset. But didn't want Reema to know that. "I'm okay, *Bhabhi*. Planning to go to sleep." She yawned loudly for Reema's benefit. "Quite a tiring day, wasn't it?"

"Yeah, I know. Rahul said that he'll talk to you as soon as he gets back." Reema paused for a moment, wondering whether she should insist on Meghna opening the door and checking out the situation for herself. But she thought better of it. Meghna sounded calm. It seemed that Reema was making a mountain out of a molehill. Anyway, there appeared to be no problem that couldn't be solved in the morning.

"Okay then, Meghna, Goodnight. Sanjay has gone on the late-night Dubai flight. Departure at two ten." She added for her sister-in-law's benefit before moving away from the door.

"Goodnight, *Bhabhi*," came the reply from beyond the still closed door.

Meghna waited for Reema's footsteps to fade away from her door before giving vent to the dry sobs tearing at her throat. Just an hour back she had been in Seventh Heaven.

Her dreams had been broken to smithereens in no time at all. How could Rahul do this to her? He had declared undying love! So where did this paramour spring from? She could have understood if he had mentioned that he had had lovers in the past. He was above thirty, after all. She was not so unreasonable, was she? But… this affair seemed to belong to the present. Meghna shuddered at the thought that Rahul had walked out of this Aisha's arms in London to step directly into hers, in Mumbai. Creep! Scoundrel! How could he do this to her? Temper clouded her brain. She didn't give him the benefit of doubt.

She felt like a wounded animal. Her pain was too great to be borne alone. She wanted her brother. Tears flowed down her face as she thought of Sanjay. Her adoring sibling who would be shocked to learn what a rat his friend actually was! She wanted the protection of his arms. She wanted him to wipe her pain away as only he knew how. He had always loved, cherished, and protected her from all her problems.

I need my brother, she thought desperately. She didn't wait as she quickly pulled off her gown and pulled on a pair of jeans and t-shirt. She stepped out of her high-heeled shoes, dragging the silver combs from her hair, brushing it hard before tying it up in a high pony. She pulled out her earrings, necklace and armlet and threw them into the dressing table drawer. She went into the bathroom and washed her face clean. As she soaped her face, she caught sight of the opal ring flashing on the ring finger of her left hand. Her engagement ring! She gave her image a bitter smile. What a farce!

She washed her face and towelled it dry. She stepped out of her bathroom, removed her ring, and gazed at it with tears in her eyes. She pressed it to her lips as she recalled the scene when Rahul had put it on her finger. That was only for a few seconds. Anger sparked in her eyes as she placed the ring on her dressing table, none too gently. She pulled out a small overnight bag and threw a couple of t-shirts and a pair of jeans in along with some bras and panties.

She was glad Sanjay was flying. She would join him on his flight and return with him after two days, by which time things would have blown over. Luckily for her Sanjay had removed a visa for her to go to Dubai with him that very month. He had promised her a shopping spree. That was before Rahul had landed on them unexpectedly.

Tears welled in her eyes once again. But she wiped them away angrily with the back of her hand.

She admonished herself saying that she had had a lucky escape. She had only got engaged to the trickster; not married him.

Meghna raised her chin in defiance and looked at her watch. 12.15 am. Reema must be in bed. She was about to step out of her room when her conscience made her scribble a note on a piece of paper for her precious *bhabhi* before placing it on the dressing table and weighing it down with the opal ring. She left the flat quietly for the international airport.

Rahul drove the car out of the gates with Aisha in the passenger seat. "Where to?" he growled.

The Leela Kempinski! She named a hotel that Rahul recognised to be near the international airport. Rahul cursed colourfully as he realised that it should take him at least an hour to drop her there and return home. He was very much tempted to dump her in a cab. But the innate sense of chivalry his father had instilled in him didn't allow him to leave a lady out on the streets, so late at night. *That is, if you could call Aisha a lady,* he thought angrily. And then there was the chance that she might not go back to the hotel but remain right here in Sion.

He turned to look at her. She had settled down comfortably against the cushioned upholstery of the passenger seat, seemingly unaware of the upheaval she had created. "What brings you here?" Rahul asked, his curiosity tickled.

"Why? You, of course, Rahul darling," she drawled in reply, fluttering her false lashes at him.

Rahul gave her a sceptical glance before turning his attention back to his driving. "Either something's wrong with my hearing or you've gone crazy."

"Not at all, Rahul dear. You heard right. And yes, you're also right that I've gone crazy. I'm crazy, about you," said Aisha, her intense gaze fixed on him.

He frowned, his eyebrows meeting in the blackest scowl. "Aisha," he said quietly, not wanting to hurt her more than was necessary. "I made it very clear to you the last time we met that I'm not interested. I've not changed my mind since," he declared.

"Come on, Rahul. Don't be shy. Your mother did warn me that it might be difficult to convince you. She was so right." Aisha had a look of rapture on her face as she spoke about Rajni. "Imagine, we'll make such a beautiful pair. We'll storm the London society."

Rahul shuddered at the mental pictures conjured by his vivid imagination, just as they reached the gates of The Leela.

He stopped the car at the entrance and opened the passenger door from inside, without getting out of his own seat. "Listen to me, Aisha and this is final. I'm not and never was interested in marrying you or spending the rest of my life with you," he bit out. "I…"

"Have your fling with that immature kid for all you want, Rahul dear," Aisha granted her permission very generously, her hand caressing the sleeve of his dress shirt. "I do understand that men's needs are different from ours. But…"

Rahul cursed under his breath before getting out of the car swiftly. He yanked the passenger door open and pulled Aisha out unceremoniously. He opened the back door and removing her baggage, thrust it into her arms before shutting both the doors violently.

"Just get out of my life and stay out. One more step from you that's out of turn and I wouldn't think twice before having the law behind you for harassment," he threatened quietly before getting into the car and riding away in a cloud of exhaust.

His quiet words more than anything else convinced Aisha that he meant what he said. She shrugged her shoulders philosophically before stepping inside the hotel. A diabolical smile split her face as she recalled Meghna's expression before she had run away from the scene. Rahul was going to have the devil's own time convincing the other woman of his innocence. *Well, life isn't so bad after all,* thought Aisha to herself. Her trip to India was obviously not the total waste she had thought it was. A sigh escaped her as she thought of the man who had got away as she went up the lift to her room.

17

"**T**his is Captain Rathod speaking…"

'Hey, that's not Sanjay,' thought Meghna, pressing the overhead button for the air hostess. When there was no response, she called out to the one who was standing further down the aisle.

"Yeh lady, shut your bloody trap or I'll blow your brains out." Meghna was horrified to hear the extremely rude voice next to her ear as she felt something metallic press against her temple.

Could it be… could it be… oh no! It *was* the muzzle of a gun, the light glinting against the metallic sheen. She was terrified to see the unkempt man holding it against her. If his voice had been guttural and grating, his face was worse. He wore his hair long and he had a thick moustache and beard. He was awfully filthy and she wouldn't have been surprised if she had seen lice crawling all over that hair.

She gave vent to the scream that forced its way into her throat. She just couldn't stop it. The next moment she faced the sweetness of oblivion as the terrorist hit her hard against her temple with the back of the gun.

Sanjay Srivastav's request for leave had been granted, only he had not been able to cancel this particular flight. But luckily for him, Captain Rathod had offered to take his place and now Sanjay was all set to go back home. He was eager to hear news of his sister's and best friend's engagement.

Sanjay was on his way home, planning to surprise his wife. He was smiling to himself as he thought of the way Rahul had been trying to resist the chains of matrimony. It was half an hour since he had left the airport when his cell phone rang.

Sanjay lifted it to his ear. The call was from the airport. The plane he was supposed to be piloting had been hijacked. He was shocked to hear the news. His first instinct was to call home and reassure his wife that he was safe. He looked at his watch. It was one forty-five am. He was sure that Meghna and Rahul would have just about reached home.

Reema picked up the phone on the fourth ring. It did not seem like her night for sleep. First it had been Aisha's visit and now the phone.

"Hello Sanjay! Aren't you flying?" She asked, surprised.

"Hi, darling. Did I wake you?"

"Mmm." Reema stretched. "You did. But anyway, tell me. Where are you? Has your flight been delayed?"

"No, my darling. I pulled out at the last minute. And I just got to know that the plane has been hijacked."

"What?" screeched Reema. She closed her eyes for a moment in silent prayer. "Sanjay…" her voice came out in a weak whisper. Although she felt sorry for the pilot who had taken her husband's place, she couldn't help feeling glad it wasn't him on the wretched flight.

"Relax, darling. I just called to tell you I'm safe. I'm going back to the airport to check on things. What news about Rahul and Meghna? Are they home yet?"

"Oh, Sanjay, it's a long story. Will tell you when you get back." Reema yawned sleepily.

"Get back to sleep, love. Sorry I disturbed you."

"I'm so glad you called, Sanjay. And thank God you are safe. Love you and bye."

Reema was in for some more excitement before the night was over. The doorbell rang after about five minutes. *This must be Rahul,* she thought. She waited for a short while for Meghna to open the door. But when the doorbell chimed once again after a couple of minutes, she got off the bed, throwing a robe over her nightie and went to open the door to a highly disturbed Rahul.

"Awfully sorry, *Bhabhi.* Where's Meghna?"

"In her room. Probably fast asleep."

"Was she okay when I left?" asked Rahul anxiously, unable to forget her blanched face when Aisha had thrown herself into his arms.

"Not to worry, Rahul." Reema hid a yawn behind her fingers. "She was kind of calm about the whole thing. In fact, she reassured me that she was fine and insisted that I went to bed. Shall I make some coffee? Doesn't seem to be a night for sleep. Sanjay called a few minutes back…" But she was talking to thin air as Rahul had gone to Meghna's room.

He knocked softly on the door which opened at his slightest touch. Feeling a strong premonition of disaster, he pushed the door further to walk in. Funny! Neither the fan nor the air-conditioner was on. He switched on the light to find the bed empty, the covers undisturbed. Could she be in the bathroom? "Meghna," he called softly. No response. "Meghna," his voice rose as panic squeezed his heart in his chest, his breathing disturbed.

He had inadvertently switched on the fan when he had put on the light. A paper fluttered in the sudden draught of air caused by the fan. He picked it off the dressing table where it had been weighted down by the engagement ring he had given Meghna that very evening. He didn't like what he saw. The note said:

Bhabhi dear,

I'm joining Sanjay on his flight to Dubai tonight. Don't worry about me. I'm perfectly fine. I just feel this tremendous need to get away. Everything's over between Rahul and me as you saw for yourself. I will be back with Sanjay. I hope that Rahul leaves town by then.

Love you, Meghna

"Goddammit," swore Rahul with a vengeance. This was what he had been afraid of. Her mood hadn't been alright when he left the flat with Aisha. But then, he hadn't wanted to discuss anything in front of the other woman. Rahul swore again as he left Meghna's bedroom, closing the door behind him with a crash.

Reema gave him a startled glance as she saw him storming out of her sister-in-law's bedroom. She had been sitting curled up on the sofa waiting to have coffee with the two of them.

"The little fool. Why couldn't she have waited for me to return? A couple of hours I turn my back and she ups and leaves. Don't I deserve a hearing at all? Do I get hung without even getting a chance to explain myself?" Rahul ranted and raved, his frustration building up by the second.

"Rahul," Reema's voice was confused. "What's it? Is Meghna asleep?"

"Asleep my foot. Please read this, *Bhabhi.*" He thrust Meghna's note close to Reema's face.

"But…" Reema had a bewildered look on her face. But when she saw the black frown on Rahul's face, she buried her nose in the letter, finding it safer, only to let out a horrified shriek as she came to the end of it. "Rahul!" Her voice cracked as she hugged the note to herself, tears streaming down her face.

Rahul had moved to the window, wondering whether he should follow his foolish young fiancée and her brother to Dubai when he heard Reema's strangled cry.

He turned around to find the even-tempered, calm Reema in a distraught state. He rushed across to shake her hard as she tried to speak while no sound emanated from her lips. She only made a keening noise as she sobbed her heart out. He put his arms around her to pull her close. He pressed her face against his shoulder, rubbing her head roughly, hoping to calm her down. He couldn't understand what had brought on the spate of weeping.

"*Bhabhi,* please calm down." He brought his own temper and frustration under control. "I'm sure Meghna's okay. It's only two days. They'll both be back…"

Reema didn't allow Rahul to complete the sentence as she shook her head vigorously. "Rahul, Sanjay called to say that his plane was hijacked."

Rahul stared at her. Was she hallucinating? *Too many hours without sleep must have brought it on,* he thought. How could someone call from a hijacked plane? He shook himself from his reverie and spoke again softly. "*Bhabhi,* let's get this clear. Sanjay phoned?"

Reema nodded even as the tears flowed faster. Rahul was totally confused. She had been quite calm when she opened the door for him earlier. There had been no phone call since, or he would have heard the phone ring. Obviously, Sanjay had called before Rahul arrived home. What had Sanjay told his wife?

"*Bhabhi,* what did he say? That his plane has been hijacked?"

"Yes, Rahul," Reema found her voice. "Sanjay had cancelled going on the hijacked plane by chance. That's why he called to assure me that he was safe. But…"

Light dawned on Rahul's dismayed face as he understood the reason for Reema's tears. Meghna was probably on the flight which Sanjay had given a miss. A tremor ran through his body as for a moment he imagined the scene on the hijacked flight.

The phone rang as if on cue. He pressed Reema on to the sofa before running across to pick up the receiver.

It was Sanjay. "Where's Meghna?" he barked, the anxiety coming across the wires.

"Sanjay," Rahul's voice almost broke with the strain, "I think she's on that wretched flight." Panic rose in his voice as he further enquired, "Any further news?"

Sanjay's voice sounded cracked as his hopes died with Rahul's answer. "Nothing good. They're terrorists, I believe. They're keeping us in suspense until further notice."

"Tell me exactly where you are. I'm coming over." Rahul turned to look at Reema pathetically as he listened to Sanjay's instructions before disconnecting the phone.

"You go ahead, Rahul," said Reema with false bravado. "I'll be fine. I'll pray for Meghna's safety." She gave him a small reassuring smile that didn't quite reach her eyes.

Rahul popped into his room to change out of his formal wear into a pair of jeans and t-shirt and left the flat, closing the door quietly behind him.

eghna woke up with a pounding headache. It was dark inside the plane with minimum lighting. She closed her eyes tightly to get her bearings while she felt her temple with her right hand. A trickle of blood had dried up and her hair was plastered to the spot. *Why haven't I died?* was her first thought. But then she was no defeatist. She recalled the incident which had led to her blacking out. She looked around slowly, her heart beating hard. Rahul's betrayal was the foremost thought in her mind despite the terrible circumstances she found herself in.

She realised that the aircraft was still. All the passengers were in their seats, quiet. Some were awake, looking frightened out of their wits while the others were asleep, although just. But no one moved. All this Meghna noticed without raising her head too much. That one beating was enough for a lifetime.

Two wild looking men were walking up and down the aisle, their rifles raised on their shoulders, a fearful sight. Somewhere a baby cried and the mother hushed it up in a hurry.

They appeared to be terrorists and seemed to be playing a waiting game. Meghna looked at her watch surreptitiously. It was past 5.30 in the morning. They should have landed at Dubai airport at 3.50 IST. But they were obviously in the middle of nowhere.

She wondered where Sanjay was. Somebody else was apparently piloting the aircraft. Reema had specifically mentioned this flight. Meghna shook her head in confusion.

Her thoughts switched to Rahul. She automatically straightened her shoulders even in her crouched position. She wondered whether he was still with that Aisha, in her hotel bedroom. She tortured herself with the visions the thought conjured up. How could he do this to her?

Her eyes misted over as she thought about their candlelight dinner. She had been on top of the world. And Rahul! Rahul had seemed so much in love with her. Was it possible for someone to fake the kind of love he had shown her that evening? He was evidently an excellent actor. He had even planned their wedding to the T.

Why had Rahul never said anything about Aisha? Meghna couldn't recall his ever mentioning the name. *Maybe because he hadn't felt her worthy of mention,* said a small voice from deep within her. She squashed the voice ruthlessly. She preferred to believe her own eyes. She had seen the way Aisha had thrown herself into Rahul's arms. She had done it with the total ease of familiarity. And Rahul had not exactly protested. Meghna could recollect clearly that he had placed his hands on the other woman's shoulders. And nobody would be foolish enough to come down to Mumbai all the way from London if she hadn't been sure of her lover. Meghna added two and two and arrived at twenty-two.

How he had wooed her so patiently, teasing and cajoling her along the way, while he had appeared to be fighting his reluctance at commitment! Meghna's face reddened as she recalled the lecture she had read him on trust and faith. Maybe he had been laughing at her all along.

In a way, Meghna was better off than her fellow passengers who were getting damn frantic with the passage of time. Meghna was totally immune to the tension surrounding her, as she was in a special kind of hell which was created by her overactive imagination.

Rahul and Sanjay shared yet another cup of tepid coffee as the minutes crawled by. It was ten am. Eight hours since the flight had been hijacked. They had stopped talking altogether, each man in his own hell.

Sanjay kept answering Reema's calls patiently, which came in every half an hour, reassuring her that no news was good news. Reema blamed herself totally. Her instinct the earlier night had been to check on Meghna personally. If she had but seen Meghna's face once, she would have realised that something was amiss. But she had taken her sister-in-law at her word. How she wished… to no avail. It was all water under the bridge. It was too late now to brood over the *ifs* and *might have beens*.

Rahul was angry first with Aisha for coming over and spoiling his life. Secondly, he blamed himself for escorting her to her hotel without talking to Meghna first. But—he swore virulently; he didn't seem to be doing much else—he had believed that Meghna was home anyway and safe. He was going to return in a couple of hours and explain the whole thing. And he had returned, just as he had planned, only to find her gone.

She knew that he had always loved her. He had even told her so that very evening, dammit. Didn't she have any faith in him? What of the lecture she had read him on faith and trust? Rahul's eyes glittered with anger and frustration. They were bloodshot from the lack of sleep and the nagging fear over Meghna's dire straits.

He turned around to look at Sanjay, his closest friend and Meghna's brother. His heart went out to him. He went over and put his arm around Sanjay's sagging shoulders and said, "Don't worry, Sanjay. I'm sure she's alright."

Sanjay raised his troubled dark eyes to his friend. "Do you think so? We have to live in hope, I suppose. Little impetuous fool! Couldn't she have had a little more trust in human beings? She thought that you, Rahul, that you, of all people, who would betray her. How stupid could she get?" His eyes were damp with unshed tears. The anxiety was beginning to tell on his face. "Her flight was totally unnecessary. How I wish she had met me! I'd have slapped some sense into her." Sanjay was anxious and at the same time furious with his sister.

Meghna suddenly felt the man on her left get up. *What is wrong with him?* As she had got into her seat just before the flight took off, she had noticed that he must be in his late forties and extremely fit for his age. Now she was horrified that he was drawing attention towards them. Was he trying to commit suicide and get her also killed in the process?

Meghna pressed her hand on his arm, trying to make him sit before one of the hijackers noticed him. But she was too late. The terrorist who had hit her mercilessly moved towards them in a flash. She closed her eyes tightly and bent her head, not wanting to be a part of the skirmish which was bound to follow.

"Please," the passenger's voice was soft and pacifying. "Allow me to go to the toilet. I'm a diabetic, you see. I don't have a lot of control over my bladder." He spoke in a gentle tone of voice.

The terrorist considered him for a couple of seconds, obviously wondering whether to trust him. Meghna's eyes had popped open the moment the other man had claimed to be a diabetic. The most important thing that had struck her about him was his athletic, well-muscled figure. She mentally shrugged her shoulders. *There was no telling anything,* she supposed. Diabetes would have been the last thing she would have associated with this particular gentleman.

The terrorist said, "Wait," in a guttural voice, pressing his rifle against the passenger's arm. He threatened him with his eyes before walking away to talk to his colleague. He came back after a minute and gave a nod, watching the man get up from his seat.

"Thank you very much," said the quiet voice before the man walked towards the toilet at the front of the plane, the terrorist holding the rifle at his back.

After a couple of minutes, there was the sound of a scuffle and a gunshot rented the air. Pandemonium broke out as children and women screamed in fear. The second terrorist rushed to the toilet where the diabetic passenger had been lying in wait for him after having shot the first one. He hit the terrorist hard on the head.

The diabetic's associate stepped out of the other toilet where he had successfully outwitted the third and last one of the trio. The two men shook hands before calming down the passengers.

"Everything is under control. Please relax. I'm Pratik Vora from the CBI and this is my colleague Jaswant Patel." Jaswant Patel moved towards the pilot's cabin to impart the good news to Captain Rathod so that he could announce it to the airports at Mumbai and Dubai. Pratik Vora continued to speak, "We were never in any real danger. We were aware of these men's activities and had been lying in wait trying to catch them red-handed. You'll agree with me when I say that 'what of a few hours of anxiety to the passengers and their relatives when we could crack down on a major terrorist gang?'" The passengers cheered him on, totally relieved after the trauma of the past eight hours. "I'm extremely sorry for all the inconvenience caused." He smiled at everyone before walking towards his seat next to Meghna.

She put her hand out to shake his enthusiastically. "Meghna Srivastav. Extremely pleased to make your acquaintance, Mr. Vora. I never did believe you were a diabetic. You appear too fit, you know."

He grinned at her as the seat belt sign came on while Captain Rathod announced the take off. They were going back to Mumbai as they were only half an hour away from there.

"I did realise that I was stretching it a bit, but I couldn't think of any other alternative," Pratik Vora replied. He had made his strategy on the go.

Meghna chatted with him, non-stop, hiding her nervousness on hearing that they were going back to Mumbai. She was glad that she could return to her brother. But Rahul would also be there. And she never wanted to set eyes on him.

Pratik Vora wondered at the sudden fire in his co-passenger's beautiful eyes and felt rather sorry for the poor man who would be at the receiving end of this young woman's temper.

They touched down at the Chhatrapati Shivaji International Airport shortly. Meghna got out of the flight the soonest as women and children were given preference. Sanjay was waiting right outside and caught her in a bear hug.

At last! He kissed his little sister on her forehead before she buried her face in his shoulder, hugging him tightly in relief. He put his hand under her chin, raising her face to check for any ravages and was shocked to see her blood-streaked temple. "Meghna."

Meghna pressed her fingers to his lips, effectively shutting him up. "That was nothing, Sanjay. A little bit of physical pain. I could take it quite easily." Her grey eyes were dull with bitterness. "It was inflicted by a total stranger, a terrorist. It's no big deal. But the pain your best friend has inflicted on my heart," tears coursed down her cheeks as she recalled the events of last night, for the millionth time, it seemed. She shook her head. "I don't think I'll ever heal."

"You idiot, Meghna. How could you ever think that Rahul of all people..."

"Thanks, Sanjay, but no, thanks. Let me handle my love affairs. I'm sure at least you're convinced that I'm man enough for that." Rahul stepped forward from where he had been standing a few feet away, giving Sanjay a chance to reunite with his sister. He couldn't help but overhear their conversation. So! She preferred the terrorist's behaviour to his, did she? A light of battle entered his golden-brown eyes.

"Did you hear that, Sanjay?" asked Meghna, triumphant. Sanjay looked down at his sister, wondering what she was gloating about. His brow cleared when she continued, "He said love affairs, in the plural."

"Meghna, I'm sure that was just a figure of speech…"

Rahul interrupted his friend once again. "Please, Sanjay. Allow me to deal with this."

Sanjay put one arm around Meghna and the other around Rahul. "I'll let the two of you deal with your difference of opinion. To be fair to Rahul, I don't think it's right for me to interfere, Meghna. Let's go home. Reema has been tearing her hair out with worry." They had reached the Fortuner when Sanjay's mobile rang yet again. "Here, speak to your *bhabhi*."

"*Bhabhi*," squealed Meghna. "I'm perfectly alright. How are you? And Sasha and Rehaan? What? You feel that I've made a mistake where Rahul is concerned?" Meghna deliberately misunderstood Reema's comment. "Of course, you're right, *Bhabhi*. I've committed a grave mistake."

Sanjay saw his friend's face tightening with temper on hearing Meghna's words. He gestured to his sister to give the cell phone to him.

"Reema, the battery's running out, love. Get the kids to the babysitters for a few hours. You and I will hit the sack when I get home. I'm sure Rahul can handle his fiancée without any help from either of us."

Meghna stamped her foot hard. "Sanjay, you're treating me like an imbecile…"

"You said it, my dear sis," said Sanjay as he lifted her bodily on to the passenger side before moving to the driver's seat. She was glaring at her brother when she felt herself being pushed to the centre of the front seat as Rahul settled on her left. She refused to meet his eyes as he put his arm on the back of the seat, his hard thigh pressed against her own soft one. She refused to acknowledge the sensations the physical contact brought forth in her body. And Sanjay! What was wrong with her brother today? He was driving the four-wheeler as if the devil was on his tail. He seemed not to miss a single pothole along the way. The car kept jerking and swerving and Meghna felt the imprint of Rahul's body throughout the ride which lasted for the better part of an hour. She didn't have any space to move into. The couple of inches that she shifted made no difference. Rahul simply moved closer. She refused to even look in his direction. Traitor!

They reached home and Reema opened the door the instant the bell rang and hugged her sister-in-law. "What a fright you gave us, Meghna!" She turned towards the men, "Let me get some coffee for all of you."

"There's no need for that, love. I don't need any just now and I hope you've already had some. You're looking as haggard as I feel. Come along. Let's go to bed," said Sanjay, throwing an arm around his wife's shoulders.

"Yeah, but what about Meghna and Rahul?"

"I'm sure they can manage to get themselves a cup of coffee, eh, Rahul?" he winked at his friend. He just wanted to give Rahul and Meghna the privacy they needed to thrash out their differences. He literally dragged his wife away from the hall.

"Not so fast," snarled Rahul as Meghna rushed into her room and tried to close the door on his face. He stopped her in time, just. He had his shoe-clad foot right between the door and the entrance to her bedroom. He thrust the door open and stepping into the room, closed it and turned the lock behind him.

"Now tell me; what's your problem?" he asked his errant fiancée.

Meghna refused to meet Rahul's eyes. "Just get out of my room, will you? I don't want you here. I hate you; do you hear? I hate you," she screamed at him as he stepped towards her; though she refused to back away, not wanting to show any fear.

Which suited Rahul just fine. He stepped forward and suddenly pulling her into his arms, kissed her full on her lips.

Meghna bunched her hands into fists but she couldn't hit him as her fists were imprisoned between her own body and the hard wall of his chest. She raised her foot and kicked him hard, on his shin.

Rahul swore yet another time. "You little hell cat. I'll…"

"How dare you? *How dare you?* You do have some guts kissing me after just stepping out of that… of that woman's arms. Just who do you think you are? You two-timing…"

Rahul shut her up once again in the only way he knew best. This time Meghna's mouth had been open and she didn't know what hit her—the sensations he created while exploring the secret corners of her mouth, the feelings only he could invoke in her. Rahul! The only man for her. Meghna melted in his arms as she slid her own around his waist.

The kiss seemed to last a lifetime before Rahul finally lifted his head.

Meghna had no fight left in her. She buried her face in his broad shoulder. She marvelled at herself. This man had betrayed her barely a couple of hours after she accepted his engagement ring. Here she was back in his arms without so much as a protest. Was she so crazy? She realised that that was true. She was totally crazy about him.

Rahul nuzzled her jaw line and moving his lips slowly, reached her ear. He took great joy in tormenting her by exploring every inch of her shell-like ear with the tip of his tongue.

Meghna purred in delight.

"Tell me something, honey. Do you really believe that I could step directly into someone's arms after the evening we spent together?" asked Rahul softly.

Meghna's head came up swiftly as her grey gaze met his honey brown one. It was hard to say who was more shocked.

Rahul drew his breath in a hiss as he noticed her face at close quarters for the first time. "That bruise looks bad, my love." He touched a finger to it gently, his face concerned. "Does it hurt badly?"

Her grey eyes were dull with pain.

He realised that he must have inadvertently inflicted that on her. "Meghna." His voice throbbed with the love that gushed forth from the bottom of his heart.

Meghna was appalled to see his blood-shot eyes. His face looked ragged after the sleepless night of anxiety. He didn't look like a man who had just stepped out of his lover's arms after a night full of fun and sex. She felt contrite. "Not now, Rahul. Not after you stroked it."

Rahul pressed his lips gently to her wound, trying to absorb some of her pain.

Meghna wrapped her arms around Rahul's neck and hung on to him as if her life depended on it. "Love me, Rahul, please," she begged. "It's my heart which is hurting, so much." She looked up at Rahul who was gazing down at her intensely.

Rahul pushed his hand under Meghna's t-shirt to press it against her heart. She drew her breath in a long sigh before pressing her body against his hand. Rahul cupped the soft mound of her breast and squeezed it gently. Her heart beat faster. He took her lips in a heart-breaking kiss before saying, "Does that feel better?"

"Yes," moaned Meghna, nodding her head in a daze. "Much better. Please don't stop." His caresses had an analgesic effect on her pain filled senses.

Meghna pulled open the couple of buttons on Rahul's t-shirt to press her lips against his throat. But after a moment, she made a frustrated sound as it kept getting in the way of her lips.

"Just a second," Rahul gave her a weak grin before yanking the t-shirt over his head.

Meghna clung to his bare torso, pressing her lips wherever she could reach and for once Rahul didn't stop her.

He made to pull Meghna's top away when she looked at him with her panic filled gaze. Rahul raised his eyebrow in enquiry. She buried her face in his chest, unable to meet his fiery golden-brown gaze.

"Please, Rahul."

"Please what? Take it off or not?" asked Rahul, his voice not quite steady, his feverish hands running over the bare skin of her waist.

There was not a peep from Meghna.

"Meghna honey," Rahul spoke softly in her ear. "You haven't answered me."

She looked up at Rahul, a hint of fear of the unknown in her passion glazed eyes. "I don't know."

Rahul respected her state of indecision and gave her a weak smile. He sat on her bed, leaning against the headboard as he pulled her into his lap.

"I love you, Meghna. Please don't ever forget that. It wasn't at all necessary for you to run away. I never was interested in Aisha. She and my mother cooked up something between the two of them and she simply landed here in Mumbai. You and I had such a wonderful evening. How could you take off after that?" Rahul asked softly as he explored every inch of her face with his lips.

Meghna gave a sigh of contentment before telling him her tale of woe. "I died a slow death when Aisha kissed you the way she did. And you didn't seem to object at all." Meghna's voice shook as she recollected the painful incident yet again. The words flowed continuously, like a river in spate.

He let her talk, his hand winnowing through her hair, the continuous caress soothing her agitation by and by.

"You put your hands on her shoulders and I didn't want to see any more." Meghna raised accusing eyes to Rahul's face.

"But, honey, if only you'd waited a few seconds longer, you'd have noticed that I placed my hands on Aisha's shoulders to push her away. I told Reema *Bhabhi* to inform you that I'll drop Aisha at her hotel and return to you."

"She told me that. I thought that Aisha mattered to you more than I did." Meghna was nothing if not honest.

Rahul chucked a fist under her chin to look into her eyes as he asked, "Would you love or marry a man who'd just dump a woman alone on the road in a strange country in the middle of the night?"

Meghna couldn't argue with his logic.

"My first instinct was to rush to you, love. But Aisha's middle name is trouble with a capital T. I wanted her far away from us more than anything else. And I thought that since you'd spoken so much to me on trust and faith going hand-in-hand together with love, I could rely on you to have faith in my love for you." Rahul punctuated every sentence with a kiss.

Meghna pressed her face into the hollow of his shoulder in shame. She understood that she had been foolish in suspecting Rahul's motives. She could now comprehend her brother's anger towards her. He definitely had more trust in his friend than she had had in the man she loved.

She lifted tortured eyes to Rahul's face. She was astonished at his patience and perseverance. Somehow, she had never associated those qualities with him.

"Rahul," her voice came out in a croak. "Rahul," she said loudly. "Can you ever forgive me? I am awfully so…"

Her lips were taken in the sweetest kiss she had ever tasted. And she should know since she had taken her lessons from an expert. Meghna clung to Rahul, desperately.

He lifted his head to glance down at her gently, "No please, sorry or thank you between lovers," he ordered authoritatively. He smiled at the woman who had stolen his heart for good.

Meghna nodded shyly, colour flaring in her cheeks.

Rahul removed the ring from where he had tucked it in his pocket and put it once again on her finger. "This time it stays," he admonished. "Any problem you have, talk it out with me straight. We're friends first, okay?"

Meghna nodded once again. He removed the other gift package he had placed under her pillow before they had left for their fateful dinner. Meghna looked at him enquiringly. "This is for you. I'd like you to wear it at our wedding."

She opened the parcel slowly, her face solemn. She gasped loudly when she saw the necklace, earrings and bracelet of opals and diamonds that Rahul had bought specially for her.

"And later, only these for our wedding night," Rahul whispered wickedly in her ear.

Meghna felt her face catch fire at the passion in his voice.

"I was going to give it to you when we reached home last night," he sighed.

Meghna raised her head to press her lips against his hair-roughened cheek. "I promise you that I'll make it up to you, Rahul. I'll be a good wife to you and I also promise to always trust you," she said sweetly.

"Did I say wedding? That was a mistake." The golden-brown eyes laughed at her startled face.

"But then who else will make an honest man of you especially now that Aisha has dumped you?"

Rahul's shoulders shook with silent laughter at her quick comeback.

"And I hope you remember that warning I'd given you on becoming *too much*?"

"Only too well. Just show me how," he invited.

Meghna did, to Rahul's absolute delight.

THE END

OTHER BOOKS
BY
SUNDARI
VENKATRAMAN

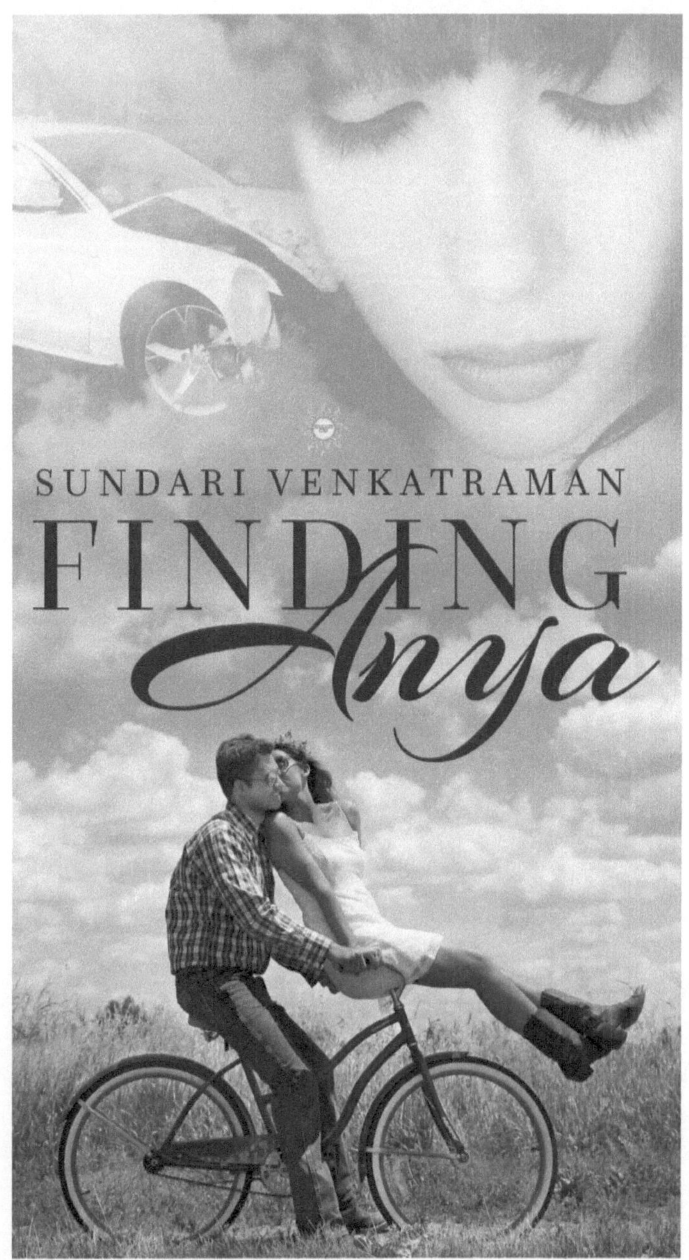
SUNDARI VENKATRAMAN
FINDING Anya

Anya Chhabria wakes up in a hospital room with no recognition of who she is and where she belongs. In her troubled times, Anya finds her anchor in a handsome stranger. But is he really unknown to her?

Dev Wadhwa's past finds him when he sees Anya lying unconscious in the middle of the road. Not willing to let go of her one more time, Dev takes her to the hospital and later to his farmhouse, where he helps her recuperate.

Sparks fly and Dev and Anya fall for each other! But the feisty Anya refuses to commit herself to marriage as her loss of memory looms larger than life.

Things aren't easy with an ex-husband, not-so-understanding parents, and a jealous neighbour thrown into the mix. What if Anya's memory never comes back?

Will Dev and Anya get a second chance?

Or will circumstances force them apart, yet again?

AN
Autograph
FOR ANJALI
SUNDARI VENKATRAMAN

At 39, Anjali Mathur feels like an exotic bird trapped in a golden cage, hating the life of the idle wife of a multi-millionaire husband who simply has neither the time nor the inclination to give her his attention.

She meets Parth at a common friend's party. It's not just his looks that Anjali's attracted to, but his gentle and understanding nature.

At 42, Parth Bhardwaj is an internationally famous author, writing under a pseudonym. Always having steered clear of married women, he has a difficult time keeping away from Anjali, feeling drawn to her from the moment he sets eyes on her.

Just when the two finally realise that they are meant for each other, the unthinkable happens.

Jayant Mathur is found murdered in his bed, making both Parth and Anjali the prime suspects.

Will Anjali ever find happiness in her lonely life?

SUNDARI
VENKATRAMAN
AMAZON BESTSELLING AUTHOR
Arjun's
PENANCE

Young Arjun feels betrayed and heartbroken when his girlfriend of two years dies in an accident. In the moment of agony, he does the worst thing possible…

Ten years later, Kiara walks into the office of the Mathur Group of industries, falling for its managing director, Arjun Mathur, who is a ruthless businessman nowadays, and also completely sworn off women.

While the ethical hacker gathers evidence against the ex-finance director of the company who has been swindling money bigtime, she tries to woo the MD into falling in love with her.

Will Kiara be able to persuade Arjun to break his penance?

Connect with Sundari Venkatraman here:

Sundari Venkatraman Books

Sundari Venkatraman Books

https://www.sundarivenkatraman.in

Author Sundari Venkatraman

@sundarivenkat

@sundarivenkatraman

sundarivenkat@gmail.com

www.ingramcontent.com/pod-product-compliance
Lightning Source LLC
Chambersburg PA
CBHW060530160726
47991CB00001B/254